EGGS, BEANS AND CRUMPETS

WHAT THIS STORY IS ABOUT

In the heart of London's clubland there stands a tall and grimly forbidding edifice known to taxi-drivers and the elegant young men who frequent its precincts as the Drones Club. Yet its somewhat austere exterior belies the atmosphere of cheerful optimism and bonhomie that prevails within. For here it is that young gallants of Mayfair forgather for the pre-luncheon bracer and to touch lightly on the topics of the day. But all is not idle chatter that passes at this hour of the morning snifter —life in its sterner aspects often comes under review and is discussed with a candour that loosens tongues and encourages confidences.

Then it is that the Eggs and Beans cluster round, and, with bated breath, listen while a Crumpet holds the floor with a dramatic narrative of domestic disturbances in the life of Bingo Little or, perhaps, the heart-throb story of Freddie Fitch-Fitch at Droitgate Spa. To the members of the Drones such epics are history in the making; and to us, because our ribs ache from joyous laughter, they are no less significant.

Eggs, Beans and Crumpets is vintage Wodehouse—an unbroken succession of uproarious chuckles that persists long after the final page has been reached.

For other books by P. G. Wodehouse see pages 285–288.

EGGS, BEANS AND CRUMPETS

by

P. G. WODEHOUSE

HERBERT JENKINS LIMITED
3 DUKE OF YORK STREET, ST. JAMES'S
LONDON, S.W.1

A
HERBERT
JENKINS'
BOOK

First printing 1940

Printed in Great Britain by
Wyman & Sons, Ltd., London, Fakenham and Reading.

CONTENTS

ALL'S WELL WITH BINGO

ALL'S WELL WITH BINGO

A BEAN and a Crumpet were in the smoking-room of the Drones Club having a quick one before lunch, when an Egg who had been seated at the writing-table in the corner rose and approached them.

"How many 'r's' in 'intolerable'?" he asked.

"Two," said the Crumpet. "Why?"

"I am writing a strong letter to the Committee," explained the Egg, "drawing their attention to the intolerable . . . Great Scot!" he cried, breaking off. "There he goes again!"

A spasm contorted his face. Outside in the passage a fresh young voice had burst into a gay song with a good deal of vo-de-o-de-o about it. The Bean cocked an attentive ear as it died away in the direction of the dining-room.

"Who is this linnet?" he inquired.

"Bingo Little, blast him. He's always singing nowadays. That's what I'm writing my strong letter to the Committee about—the intolerable nuisance of this incessant heartiness of his. Because it isn't only his singing. He slaps backs. Only yesterday he came sneaking up behind me in the bar and sloshed me between the shoulder-blades, saying 'Aha!' as he did so. Might have choked me. How many 's's' in 'incessant'?"

"Three," said the Crumpet.

"Thanks," said the Egg.

He returned to the writing-table. The Bean seemed perplexed.

"Odd," he said. "Very odd. How do you account for young Bingo carrying on like this?"

"Just *joie de vivre*."

"But he's married. Didn't he marry some female novelist or other?"

"That's right. Rosie M. Banks, authoress of *Only A Factory Girl*, *Mervyn Keene, Clubman*, *'Twas Once In May*, and other works. You see her name everywhere. I understand she makes a packet with the pen."

"I didn't know married men had any *joie de vivre*."

"Not many, of course. But Bingo's union has been an exceptionally happy one. He and the other half of the sketch have hit it off from the start like a couple of love-birds."

"Well, he oughtn't to slap backs about it."

"You don't know the inside facts. Bingo is no mere wanton back-slapper. What has made him that way at the moment is the fact that he recently had a most merciful escape. There was within a toucher of being very serious trouble in the home."

"But you said they were like a couple of love-birds."

"Quite. But even with love-birds circumstances can arise which will cause the female love-bird to get above herself and start throwing her weight about. If

Mrs. Bingo had got on Bingo what at one time it appeared inevitable that she must get on him, it would have kept her in conversation for the remainder of their married lives. She is a sweet little thing, one of the best, but women are women and I think that there can be no doubt that she would have continued to make passing allusions to the affair right up to the golden wedding day. The way Bingo looks at it is that he has escaped the fate that is worse than death, and I am inclined to agree with him."

The thing started one morning when Bingo returned to the love-nest for a bite of lunch after taking the Pekinese for a saunter. He was in the hall trying to balance an umbrella on the tip of his nose, his habit when at leisure, and Mrs. Bingo came out of her study with a wrinkled brow and a couple of spots of ink on her chin.

"Oh, there you are," she said. "Bingo, have you ever been to Monte Carlo?"

Bingo could not help wincing a little at this. Unwittingly, the woman had touched an exposed nerve. The thing he had always wanted to do most in the world was to go to Monte Carlo, for he had a system which couldn't fail to clean out the Casino; but few places, as you are probably aware, are more difficult for a married man to sneak off to.

"No," he said with a touch of moodiness. Then, recovering his usual sunny aplomb: "Look," he said. "Watch, old partner in sickness and in health. I place the umbrella so. Then, maintaining a perfect equilibrium . . ."

"I want you to go there at once," said Mrs. Bingo.

Bingo dropped the umbrella. You could have knocked him down with a toothpick. For a moment, he tells me, he thought that he must be dreaming some beautiful dream.

"It's for my book. I can't get on without some local colour."

Bingo grasped the gist. Mrs. Bingo had often discussed this business of local colour with him. Nowadays, he knew, if you are providing wholesome fiction for the masses, you have simply got to get your atmosphere right. The customers have become cagey. They know too much. Chance your arm with the *mise en scène*, and before you can say "What ho," you've made some bloomer and people are writing you nasty letters, beginning "Dear Madam, Are you aware——?"

"And I can't go myself. There's the Pen and Ink dinner on Friday, and on Tuesday the Writers' Club is giving a luncheon to Mrs. Carrie Melrose Bopp, the American novelist. And any moment now I shall be coming to the part where Lord Peter Shipbourne breaks the bank. So do you think you could possibly go, Bingo darling?"

Bingo was beginning to understand how the Israelites must have felt when that manna started descending in the wilderness.

"Of course I'll go, old egg," he said heartily. "Anything I can——"

His voice trailed away. A sudden thought had

come, biting into his soul like acid. He had remembered that he hadn't a bean to his name. He had lost every penny he possessed two weeks before on a horse called Bounding Beauty which was running—if you could call it running—in the two-thirty at Haydock Park.

The trouble with old Bingo is that he will allow his cooler judgment to be warped by dreams and omens. Nobody had known better than he that by the ruling of the form-book Bounding Beauty hadn't a chance: but on the eve of the race he had a nightmare in which he saw his Uncle Wilberforce dancing the rumba in the nude on the steps of the National Liberal Club and, like a silly ass, accepted this as a bit of stable information. And bang, as I say, had gone every penny he had in the world.

For a moment he reeled a bit. Then he brightened. Rosie, he reasoned, would scarcely expect him to undertake an irksome job like sweating all the way over to Monte Carlo without financing the tedious expedition.

"Of course, of course, of course," he said. "Yes, rather! I'll start to-morrow. And about expenses. I suppose a hundred quid would see me through, though two would be still better, and even three wouldn't hurt. . . ."

"Oh, no, that's all right," said Mrs. Bingo. "You won't need any money."

Bingo gulped like an ostrich swallowing a brass door-knob.

"Not . . . need . . . any . . . money?

"Except a pound or two for tips and so on. Everything is arranged. Dora Spurgeon is at Cannes, and I'm going to 'phone her to get you a room at the Hôtel de Paris at Monte Carlo, and all the bills will be sent to my bank."

Bingo had to gulp a couple more times before he was able to continue holding up his end of the duologue.

"But I take it," he said in a low voice, "that you want me to hobnob with the international spies and veiled women and so forth and observe their habits carefully, don't you? This will run into money. You know what international spies are. It's champagne for them every time, and no half-bots, either."

"You needn't bother about the spies. I can imagine them. All I want is the local colour. An exact description of the Rooms and the Square and all that. Besides, if you had a lot of money, you might be tempted to gamble."

"What!" cried Bingo. "Gamble? Me?"

"No, no," said Mrs. Bingo remorsefully. "I'm wronging you, of course. Still, I think I'd sooner we did it in the way I've arranged."

So there you have the position of affairs, and you will not be surprised to learn that poor old Bingo made an indifferent lunch, toying with the minced chicken and pushing the roly-poly pudding away untasted. His manner during the meal was distrait, for his brain was racing like a dynamo. Somehow he had got to get the stuff. But how? How?

Bingo, you see, is not a man who finds it easy to float a really substantial loan. People know too much about his financial outlook. He will have it in sack-fuls some day, of course, but until he realizes on his Uncle Wilberforce—who is eighty-six and may quite easily go to par—the wolf, so far as he is concerned, will always be in or about the vestibule. The public is aware of this, and it makes the market sluggish.

It seemed to him, brooding over the thing, that his only prospect for the sort of sum he required was Oofy Prosser. Oofy, while not an easy parter, is a millionaire, and a millionaire was what he required. So round about cocktail time he buzzed off to the club, only to be informed that Oofy was abroad. The disappointment was so severe that he was compelled to go to the smoking-room and have a restorative. I was there when he came in, and so haggard and fishlike was his demeanour that I asked him what was up, and he told me all.

"You couldn't lend me between twenty and twenty-five, or, better still, thirty quid, could you?" he said.

I said No, I couldn't, and he heaved a long, low, quivering sigh.

"And so it goes on," he said. "That's Life. Here I am with this unique opportunity of making a stu-pendous fortune, and crippled for lack of the essential capital. Did you ever hear of a chap called Garcia?"

"No."

"Skinned the Monte Carlo Administration of a hundred thousand quid in his day. Ever hear of a chap called Darnborough?"

"No."

"Eighty-three thousand of the best was what he pocketed. Did you ever hear of a chap called Owers?"

"No."

"His winning streak lasted for more than twenty years. These three birds of whom I speak simply went to Monte Carlo and lolled back in their chairs with fat cigars, and the Casino just thrust the money on them. And I don't suppose any of them had a system like mine. Oh, hell, a thousand curses," said Bingo.

Well, there isn't much you can say when a fellow's in the depths like that. The only thing I could suggest was that he should put some little trinket up the spout temporarily. His cigarette-case, for instance, I said; and it was then that I learned that that cigarette-case of his is not the solid gold we have always imagined. Tin, really. And except for the cigarette-case, it appeared, the only trinket he had ever possessed was a diamond brooch which, being in funds at the time as the result of a fortunate speculation at Catterick Bridge, he had bought Mrs. Bingo for a birthday present.

It all seemed pretty hopeless, accordingly, so I merely offered him my heartfelt sympathy and another snootful. And next morning he steamed off on the eleven o'clock express, despair in his soul and in his pocket a note-book, four pencils, his return ticket, and about three pounds for tips and so on. And shortly before lunch on the following day he was alighting at Monte Carlo station.

I don't know if you remember a song some years ago

that went "Ti-um-ti-um-ti-um-ti-um, Ti-um-ti-um-ti-ay," and then, after a bit more of that, finished up:

Ti-um-ti-um-ti-um-ti-UM,
The curse of an aching heart.

You don't hear it much nowadays, but at one time you were extraordinarily apt to get it shot at you by bassos at smoking concerts and entertainments in aid of the Church Organ Fund in the old village hall. They would pause for a moment after the "UM" and take a breath that came up from their ankle bones, and then:

It's the curse of an A-ching heart.

Most unpleasant, of course, the whole thing, and I wouldn't have mentioned it, only the phrase absolutely puts in a nutshell the way poor old Bingo felt during his first two days at Monte Carlo. He had an aching heart, and he cursed like billy-o. And I'm not surprised, poor chap, for he was suffering severe torments.

All day long, though it was like twisting the knife in the wound, he would wander through the Rooms, trying out that system of his on paper; and the more he tried it out, the more iron-clad it revealed itself. Simply couldn't lose.

By bedtime on the second night he found that, if he had been plying in hundred-franc chips, he would have been no less than two hundred and fifty pounds ahead—just like that. In short, there was all that

B

stuff—his for the picking up, as you might say—and he couldn't get it.

Garcia would have got it. Darnborough would have got it. So would Owers. But he couldn't. Simply, mark you, for lack of a trifling spot of initial capital which a fellow like Oofy Prosser could have slipped him and never felt it. Pretty bitter.

And then, on the third morning, as he sat glancing through the newspaper over the breakfast-table, he saw a news item which brought him up in his chair with a jerk, choking over his coffee.

Among the recent arrivals at the Hôtel Magnifique at Nice, it said, were Their Serene Highnesses the Prince and Princess of Graustark, His Majesty the ex-King of Ruritania, Lord Percy Poffin, the Countess of Goffin, Major-General Sir Everard Slurk, K.V.O., and Mr. Prosser.

Well, of course, it might be some other brand of Prosser, but Bingo didn't think so. An hotel where Serene Highnesses were to be found was just the place for which a bally snob like Oofy would have made a bee-line. He rushed to the telephone and was presently in communication with the concierge.

"Hullo? Yes?" said the concierge. "This is the Hôtel Magnifique. Hall porter speaking."

"*Dites-moi,*" said Bingo. "*Esker-vous avez dans votre hôtel un monsieur nommé* Prosser?"

"Yes, sir. Quite correct. There is a Mr. Prosser staying in the hotel."

"*Est-il un oiseau avec beaucoup de* . . . Oh, hell, what's the French for 'pimples'?"

"The word you are trying to find is *bouton*," said the concierge. "Yes, sir, Mr. Prosser is liberally pimpled."

"Then put me through to his room," said Bingo. And pretty soon he heard a sleepy and familiar voice hullo-ing.

"Hullo, Oofy, old man," he cried. "This is Bingo Little."

"Oh, my God!" said Oofy, and something in his manner warned Bingo that it would be well to proceed with snakiness and caution.

There were, he knew, two things which rendered Oofy Prosser a difficult proposition for the ear-biter. In the first place, owing to his habit of mopping it up at late parties, he nearly always had a dyspeptic headache. In the second place, his position as the official moneyed man of the Drones Club had caused him to become shy and wary, like a bird that's been a good deal shot over. You can't touch a chap like that on the telephone at ten in the morning. It would, he perceived, if solid results were to be obtained, be necessary to sweeten Oofy.

"I just this minute saw in the paper that you were in these parts, Oofy, old man. A wonderful surprise it was. Gosh, I said. Golly, I said. Dear old Oofy, I said. Well, well, well!"

"Get on with it," said Oofy. "What do you want?"

"Why, to give you lunch, of course, old chap," said Bingo.

Yes, he had made the great decision. That money

which he had been earmarking for tips must be diverted to another end. It might lead to his having to sneak out of the hotel at the conclusion of his visit with his face scarlet and his ears hanging down, but the risk had to be taken. Nothing venture, nothing have.

At the other end of the telephone he heard a sort of choking gasp.

"There must be something wrong with this wire," said Oofy. "It sounds just as if you were saying you want to give me lunch."

"So I am."

"*Give* me lunch?"

"That's right."

"What, pay the bill?"

"Yes."

There was a silence.

"I must send this to Ripley," said Oofy.

"Ripley?"

"The Believe-it-or-not man."

"Oh?" said Bingo. He was not quite sure that he liked Oofy's attitude, but he remained sunny. "Well, where and when? What time? What place?"

"We may as well lunch here. Come fairly early, because I'm going to the races this afternoon."

"Right," said Bingo. "I'll be on the mat at one sharp."

And at one sharp there he was, his little all in his pocket. His emotions, he tells me, as he drove in on the Monte Carlo-Nice 'bus, were mixed. One moment, he was hoping that Oofy would have his usual dyspeptic headache, because that would blunt his, Oofy's, appetite and enable him, Bingo, to save something out of the wreck: the next, he was reminding himself that an Oofy with dull, shooting pains about the temples would be less likely to come across. It was all very complex.

Well, as it turned out, Oofy's appetite was the reverse of blunted. The extraordinary position in which he found himself—guest and not host to a fellow-member of the Drones—seemed to have put an edge on it. It is not too much to say that from the very outset he ate like a starving python. The light, casual way in which he spoke to the head waiter about hot-house grapes and asparagus froze Bingo to the marrow. And when—from force of habit, no doubt—he called for the wine list and ordered a nice, dry champagne, it began to look to Bingo as if the bill for this binge was going to resemble something submitted to Congress by President Roosevelt in aid of the American Farmer.

However, though once or twice—notably when Oofy started wading into the caviare—he had to clench his fists and summon up all his iron self-control, he did not on the whole repine. Each moment, as the feast proceeded, he could see his guest becoming more and more mellow. It seemed merely a question of time before the milk of human kindness would come gushing out of him as if the dam had burst. Feeling that a cigar and liqueur ought just about to do the trick, Bingo ordered them: and Oofy, unbuttoning the last three buttons of his waistcoat, leaned back in his chair.

"Well," said Oofy, beaming, "this will certainly be something to tell my grandchildren. I mean, that I once lunched with a member of the Drones Club and didn't get stuck with the bill. Listen, Bingo, I'd like to do something for you in return."

Bingo felt like some great actor who has received his cue. He leaned forward and relighted Oofy's cigar with a loving hand. He also flicked a speck of dust off his coat-sleeve.

"And what I'm going to do is this. I'm going to give you a tip. On these races this afternoon. Back Spotted Dog for the *Prix Honore Sauvan*. A sure winner."

"Thanks, Oofy, old man," said Bingo. "That's splendid news. If you will lend me a tenner, then, Oofy, old boy, I'll put it on."

"What do you want me to lend you a tenner for?"

"Because, after I've paid the lunch bill, Oofy, old chap, I shan't have any money."

"You won't need any money," said Oofy, and Bingo wondered how many more people were going to make this blithering remark to him. "My London bookie is staying here. He will accommodate you in credit, seeing that you are a friend of mine."

"But doesn't it seem a pity to bother him with a lot of extra book-keeping, Oofy, old fellow?" said Bingo, flicking another speck of dust off Oofy's other coat-sleeve. "Much better if you would just lend me a tenner."

"Joking aside," said Oofy, "I think I'll have another kümmel."

And it was at this moment, when the conversation appeared to have reached a deadlock and there seemed no hope of finding a formula, that a stout, benevolent-looking man approached their table. From the fact that he and Oofy at once began to talk odds and figures, Bingo deduced that this must be the bookie from London.

"And my friend, Mr. Little," said Oofy, in conclusion, "wants a tenner on Spotted Dog for the *Prix Honore Sauvan.*"

And Bingo was just about to shake his head and say that he didn't think his wife would like him to bet, when the glorious Riviera sunshine, streaming in through the window by which they sat, lit up Oofy's face and he saw that it was a perfect mass of spots. A moment later, he perceived that the bookie had a pink spot on his nose and the waiter, who was now bringing the bill, a bountifully spotted forehead. A thrill shot through him. These things, he knew, are sent to us for a purpose.

"Right ho," he said. "A tenner at the current odds."

And then they all went off to the races. The *Prix Honore Sauvan* was the three o'clock. A horse called Lilium won it. Kerry second, Maubourget third, Ironside fourth, Irresistible fifth, Sweet and Lovely sixth, Spotted Dog seventh. Seven ran. So there was Bingo owing ten quid to this bookie and not a chance of a happy ending unless the fellow would consent to let the settlement stand over for a bit.

So he buttonholed the bookie and suggested this, and the bookie said "Certainly."

"Certainly," said the bookie. He put his hand on Bingo's shoulder and patted it. "I like you, Mr. Little," he said.

"Do you?" said Bingo, putting his hand on the bookie's and patting that. "Do you, old pal?"

"I do indeed," said the bookie. "You remind me of my little boy Percy, who took the knock the year Worcester Sauce won the Jubilee Handicap. Bronchial trouble. So when you ask me to wait for my money, I say of course I'll wait for my money. Suppose we say till next Friday?"

Bingo blenched a bit. The period he had had in mind had been something more along the lines of a year or eighteen months.

"Well," he said, "I'll try to brass up then . . . but you know how it is . . . you mustn't be disappointed if . . . this world-wide money shortage . . . circumstances over which I have no control . . ."

"You think you may not be able to settle?"

"I'm a bit doubtful."

The bookie pursed his lips.

"I do hope you will," he said, "and I'll tell you why. It's silly to be superstitious, I know, but I can't help remembering that every single bloke that's ever done me down for money has had a nasty accident occur to him. Time after time, I've seen it happen."

"Have you?" said Bingo, beginning to exhibit symptoms of bronchial trouble, like the late Percy.

"I have, indeed," said the bookie. "Time after

time after time. It almost seems like some kind of
fate. Only the other day there was a fellow with a
ginger moustache named Watherspoon. Owed me
fifty for Plumpton and pleaded the Gaming Act.
And would you believe it, less than a week later he
was found unconscious in the street—must have
got into some unpleasantness of some kind—and had
to have six stitches."

"Six!"

"Seven. I was forgetting the one over his left
eye. Makes you think, that sort of thing does. Hoy,
Erbut," he called.

A frightful plugugly appeared from nowhere, as if
he had been a Djinn and the bookie had rubbed a
lamp.

"Erbut," said the bookie, "I want you to meet
Mr. Little, Erbut. Take a good look at him. You'll
remember him again?"

Herbert drank Bingo in. His eye was cold and
grey, like a parrot's.

"Yus," he said. "Yus, I won't forget him."

"Good," said the bookie. "That will be all,
Erbut. Then about that money, Mr. Little, we'll
say Friday without fail, shall we?"

Bingo tottered away and sought out Oofy.

"Oofy, old man," he said, "it is within your power
to save a human life."

"Well, I'm jolly well not going to," said Oofy,
who had now got one of his dyspeptic headaches.
"The more human lives that aren't saved, the better
I shall like it. I loathe the human race. Any time

it wants to go over Niagara Falls in a barrel, it will be all right with me."

"If I don't get a tenner by Friday, a fearful bounder named Erbut is going to beat me into a pulp."

"Good," said Oofy, brightening a little. "Capital. Splendid. That's fine."

Bingo then caught the 'bus back to Monte Carlo.

That night he dressed for dinner moodily. He was unable to discern the bluebird. In three months from now he would be getting another quarter's allowance, but a fat lot of good that would be. In far less than three months, if he had read aright the message in Erbut's eyes, he would be in some hospital or nursing home with stitches all over him. How many stitches, time alone could tell. He fell to musing on Watherspoon. Was it, he wondered, to be his fate to lower that ginger-moustached man's melancholy record?

His thoughts were still busy with the stitch outlook, when the telephone rang.

"Hullo," said a female voice. "Is that Rosie?"

"No," said Bingo, and might have added that the future was not either. "I'm Mr. Little."

"Oh, Mr. Little, this is Dora Spurgeon. Can I speak to Rosie?"

"She isn't here."

"Well, when she comes in, will you tell her that I'm just off to Corsica in some people's yacht. We leave in an hour, so I shan't have time to come over and see her, so will you give her my love and tell her I am sending the brooch back."

"Brooch?"

"She lent me her brooch when I left London. I think it's the one you gave her on her birthday. She told me to take special care of it, and I don't feel it's safe having it with me in Corsica—so many brigands about—so I am sending it by registered post to the Hôtel de Paris. Good-bye, Mr. Little. I must rush."

Bingo hung up the receiver and sat down on the bed to think this over. Up to a point, of course, the situation was clear. Dora Spurgeon, a muddle-headed boob if ever there was one, obviously supposed that Mrs. Bingo had accompanied him to Monte Carlo. No doubt Mrs. Bingo had gone to some pains in her telephone call to make it thoroughly clear that she was remaining in London, but it was no good trying to drive things into a head like Dora Spurgeon's by means of the spoken word. You needed a hammer. The result was that on the morrow that brooch which he had given Mrs. Bingo would arrive at the hotel.

So far, as I say, Bingo found nothing to perplex him. But what he could not make up his mind about was this—should he, after he had pawned the brooch, send the proceeds straight to that bookie? Or should he take the money and go and have a whack at the Casino?

Far into the silent night he pondered without being able to reach a decision, but next morning everything seemed to clarify, as is so often the way after a night's sleep, and he wondered how he could ever have been in doubt. Of course he must have a whack at the Casino.

The catch about sending the money to the bookie was that, while this policy would remove from his future the dark shadow of Erbut, it would not make for contentment and happiness in the home. When Mrs. Bingo discovered that he had shoved her brooch up the spout in order to pay a racing debt, friction would ensue. He unquestionably had a moral claim on the brooch—bought with his hard-earned money— the thing, you might say, was really his to do what he liked with—nevertheless, something told him that friction would ensue.

By going and playing his system he would avoid all unpleasantness. It was simply a matter of strolling into the Rooms and taking the stuff away.

And, as it turned out, he couldn't have paid off Erbut's bookie, anyway, because the local pop-shop would only give him a fiver on the brooch. He pleaded passionately for more, but the cove behind the counter was adamant. So, taking the fiver, he lunched sparingly at a pub up the hill, and shortly after two o'clock was in the arena, doing his stuff.

I have never been able to quite get the hang of that system of Bingo's. He has explained it to me a dozen times, but it remains vague. However, the basis of it, the thing that made it so frightfully in- genious, was that instead of doubling your stake when you lost, as in all these other systems, you doubled it when you won. It involved a lot of fancy work with a pencil and a bit of paper, because you had to write down figures and add figures and scratch figures out, but that, I gathered, was the nub of the thing—you doubled up when you won, thus increasing your profits by leaps and bounds and making the authorities look pretty sick.

The only snag about it was that in order to do this you first had to win, which Bingo didn't.

I don't suppose there is anything—not even Oofy Prosser—that has a nastier disposition than the wheel at Monte Carlo. It seems to take a sinister pleasure in doing down the common people. You can play mentally by the hour and never get a losing spin, but once you put real money up the whole aspect of things alters. Poor old Bingo hadn't been able to put a foot wrong so long as he stuck to paper punting, but he now found himself in the soup from the start.

There he stood, straining like a greyhound at the leash, waiting for his chance of doubling up, only to see all his little capital raked in except one solitary hundred-franc chip. And when with a weary gesture he bunged this on Black, up came Zero and it was swept away.

And scarcely had he passed through this gruelling spiritual experience, when a voice behind him said, "Oh, there you are!" and, turning, he found himself face to face with Mrs. Bingo.

He stood gaping at her, his heart bounding about inside him like an adagio dancer with nettlerash. For an instant, he tells me, he was under the impression that this was no flesh and blood creature that stood before him, but a phantasm. He thought that she must have been run over by a 'bus or something in London and that this was her spectre looking in to report, as spectres do.

"You!" he said, like someone in a play.

"I've just arrived," said Mrs. Bingo, very merry and bright.

"I—I didn't know you were coming."

"I thought I would surprise you," said Mrs. Bingo, still bubbling over with joyous animation. "You see, what happened was that I was talking to Millie Pringle about my book, and she said that it was no use getting local colour about the Rooms, because a man like Lord Peter Shipbourne would never go to the Rooms—he would do all his playing at the Sporting Club. And I was just going to wire you to go there, when Mrs. Carrie Melrose Bopp trod on a banana-skin in the street and sprained her ankle, and the luncheon was postponed, so there was nothing to prevent me coming over, so I came. Oh, Bingo, darling, isn't this jolly!"

Bingo quivered from cravat to socks. The adjective "jolly" was not the one he would have selected. And it was at this point that Mrs. Bingo appeared to observe for the first time that her loved one was looking like a corpse that has been left out in the rain for a day or two.

"Bingo!" she cried. "What's the matter?"

"Nothing," said Bingo. "Nothing. Matter? How do you mean?"

"You look . . ." A wifely suspicion shot through

Mrs. Bingo. She eyed him narrowly. "You haven't been gambling?"

"No, no," said Bingo. He is a fellow who is rather exact in his speech, and the word "gambling," to his mind, implied that a chap had a chance of winning. All that he had done, he felt, had been to take his little bit of money and give it to the Administration. You couldn't describe that as gambling. More like making a donation to a charity. "No, no," he said. "Rather not."

"I'm so glad. Oh, by the way, I found a letter from Dora Spurgeon at the hotel. She said she was sending my brooch. I suppose it will arrive this afternoon."

Bingo's gallant spirit was broken. It seemed to him that this was the end. It was all over, he felt, except the composition of the speech in which he must confess everything. And he was just running over in his mind a few opening remarks, beginning with the words "Listen, darling," when his eye fell on the table, and there on Black was a pile of chips, worth in all no less than three thousand, two hundred francs— or, looking at it from another angle, about forty quid at that date. And as he gazed at them, wondering which of the lucky stiffs seated round the board had got ahead of the game to that extent, the croupier at the bottom of the table caught his eye and smirked congratulatingly, as croupiers do when somebody has won a parcel and they think that there is going to be something in it for them in the way of largess.

And Bingo, tottering on his base, suddenly realized

that this piled up wealth belonged to him.   It was the increment accruing from that last hundred francs of his.

What he had forgotten, you see, was that though, when Zero turns up, those who have betted on numbers, columns, and what not get it in the neck, stakes on the even chances aren't scooped up—they are what is called put in prison.   I mean, they just withdraw into the background for the moment, awaiting the result of the next spin.   And, if that wins, out they come again.

Bingo's hundred francs had been on Black, so Zero had put it in prison.   And then, presumably, Black must have turned up, getting it out again. And, as he hadn't taken it off, it had, of course, stayed on Black.   And then, while he was immersed in conversation with Mrs. Bingo about brooches, the wheel, from being a sort of mechanical Oofy Prosser, had suddenly turned into a Santa Claus.

Seven more times it had come up Black, putting Bingo in the position in which that system of his ought to have put him, viz., of doubling up when he won.   And the result, as I say, was that the loot now amounted to the colossal sum of forty quid, more than double what he required in order to be able to pay off all his obligations and look the world in the eye again.

The relief was so terrific that Bingo tells me he came within a toucher of swooning.   And it was only as he was about to snatch the stuff up and trouser it and live happily ever after—he had, indeed, actually poised himself for the spring—that he suddenly saw that there was a catch. To wit, that if he did, all must be discovered. Mrs. Bingo would know that he had been gambling, she would speedily ascertain the source whence had proceeded the money he had been gambling with, and the home, if not actually wrecked, would unquestionably become about as hot for him as the inside of a baked potato.

And yet, if he left the doubloons where they were, the next spin might see them all go down the drain.

I expect you know the expression "A man's cross-roads." Those were what Bingo was at at this juncture.

There seemed just one hope—to make a face at the croupier and do it with such consummate skill that the other would see that he wanted those thirty-two hundred francs taken off the board and put on one side till he was at liberty to come and collect. So he threw his whole soul into a face, and the croupier nodded intelligently and left the money on. Bingo, he saw, was signalling to him to let the works ride for another spin, and he admired his sporting spirit. He said something to the other croupier in an under-tone—no doubt "*Quel homme!*" or "*Epatant!*" or something of that kind.

And the wheel, which now appeared definitely to have accepted the role of Bingo's rich uncle from Australia, fetched up another Black.

Mrs. Bingo was studying the gamesters. She didn't seem to think much of them.

"What dreadful faces these people have," she said.

c

Bingo did not reply.   His own face at this moment was nothing to write home about, resembling more than anything else that of an anxious fiend in Hell.   He was watching the wheel revolve.

It came up Black again, bringing his total to twelve thousand, eight hundred.

And now at last it seemed that his tortured spirit was to be at rest.   The croupier, having shot another smirk in his direction, was leaning forward to the pile of chips and had started scooping.   Yes, all was well.   At the eleventh hour the silly ass had divined the message of that face of his and was doing the needful.

Bingo drew a deep, shuddering breath.   He felt like one who had passed through the furnace and, though a bit charred in spots, can once more take up the burden of life with an easy mind.   Twelve thousand, eight hundred francs . . .   Gosh!   It was over a hundred and fifty quid, more than he had ever possessed at one time since the Christmas, three years ago, when his Uncle Wilberforce had come over all Dickensy as the result of lemon punch and had given him a cheque on which next day he had vainly tried to stop payment.   There was a froust in the Rooms which you could have cut with a knife, but he drew it into his lungs as if it had been the finest ozone. Birds seemed to be twittering from the ceiling and soft music playing everywhere.

And then the world went to pieces again.   The wheel had begun to spin, and there on Black lay twelve thousand francs.   The croupier, though he had scooped, hadn't scooped enough. All he had done was to remove from the board the eight hundred. On that last coup, you see, Bingo had come up against the limit. You can't have more than twelve thousand on an even chance.

And, of course, eight hundred francs was no use to him whatever. It would enable him to pay off Erbut and the bookie, but what of the brooch?

It was at this point that he was aware that Mrs. Bingo was saying something to him. He came slowly out of his trance with a Where-am-I look.

"Eh?" he said.

"I said, 'Don't you think so'?"

"Think so?"

"I was saying that it didn't seem much good wasting any more time in here. Millie Pringle was quite right. Lord Peter Shipbourne would never dream of coming to a place like this. He would never stand the smell, for one thing. I have drawn him as a most fastidious man. So shall I go on to the Sporting Club . . . Bingo?"

Bingo was watching the wheel, tense and rigid. He was tense and rigid, I mean, not the wheel. The wheel was spinning.

"Bingo!"

"Hullo?"

"Shall I go on to the Sporting Club and pay our entrance fees?"

A sudden bright light came into Bingo's face, rendering it almost beautiful. His brow was bedewed with perspiration, and he rather thought his hair had turned snowy white, but the map was shining like the sun at noon, and he beamed as he had seldom beamed before.

For the returns were in. The wheel had stopped. And once again Black had come up, and even now the croupier was removing twelve thousand francs from the pile and adding them to the eight hundred before him.

"Yes, do," said Bingo. "Do. Yes, do. That'll be fine. Splendid. I think I'll just stick on here for a minute or two. I like watching these weird blokes. But you go on and I'll join you."

Twenty minutes later he did so. He walked into the Sporting Club a little stiffly, for there were forty-eight thousand francs distributed about his person, some of it in his pockets, some of it in his socks, and quite a good deal tucked inside his shirt. He did not see Mrs. Bingo at first: then he caught sight of her sitting over in the bar with a bottle of Vittel in front of her.

"What ho, what ho," he said, lumbering up.

Then he paused, for it seemed to him that her manner was rummy. Her face was sad and set, her eyes dull. She gave him an odd look, and an appalling suspicion struck him amidships. Could it be, he asked himself—was it possible that somehow, by some mysterious wifely intuition . . .

"There you are," he said. He sat down beside her, hoping that he wasn't going to crackle. "Er— how's everything?" He paused. She was still looking rummy. "I've got that brooch," he said.

"Oh?"

"Yes. I—er—thought you might like to have it, so I—ah—nipped out and got it."

"I'm glad it arrived safely . . . Bingo!" said Mrs. Bingo.

She was staring sombrely before her. Bingo's apprehension increased. He now definitely feared the worst. It was as if he could feel the soup plashing about his ankles. He took her hand in his and pressed it. It might, he felt, help. You never knew.

"Bingo," said Mrs. Bingo, "we always tell each other everything, don't we?"

"Do we? Oh, yes. Yes."

"Because when we got married, we decided that that was the only way. I remember your saying so on the honeymoon."

"Yes," said Bingo, licking his lips and marvelling at the depths of fatheadedness to which men can sink on their honeymoons.

"I'd hate to feel that you were concealing anything from me. It would make me wretched."

"Yes," said Bingo.

"So if you had been gambling, you would tell me, wouldn't you?"

Bingo drew a deep breath. It made him crackle all over, but he couldn't help that. He needed air. Besides, what did it matter now if he crackled like a forest fire? He threw his mind back to those opening sentences which he had composed.

"Listen, darling," he began.

"So I must tell you," said Mrs. Bingo. "I've

just made the most dreadful fool of myself. When I came in here, I went over to that table there to watch the play, and suddenly something came over me. . . ."

Bingo uttered a snort which rang through the Sporting Club like a bugle.

"You didn't have a pop?"

"I lost over two hundred pounds in ten minutes——Oh, Bingo, can you ever forgive me?"

Bingo had still got hold of her hand, for he had been relying on the soothing effects of hanging on to it during the remarks which he had outlined. He squeezed it lovingly. Not immediately, however, because for perhaps half a minute he felt so boneless that he could not have squeezed a grape.

"There, there!" he said.

"Oh, Bingo!"

"There, there, there!"

"You do forgive me?"

"Of course. Of course."

"Oh, Bingo," cried Mrs. Bingo, her eyes like twin stars, and damp ones at that, "there's nobody like you in the world."

"Would you say that?"

"You remind me of Sir Galahad. Most husbands——"

"Ah," said Bingo, "but I understand these sudden impulses. I don't have them myself, but I understand them. Not another word. Good gosh, what's a couple of hundred quid, if it gave you a moment's pleasure?"

His emotions now almost overpowered him, so strenuously did they call for an outlet. He wanted to shout, but he couldn't shout—the croupiers would object. He wanted to give three cheers, but he couldn't give three cheers—the barman wouldn't like it. He wanted to sing, but he couldn't sing—the customers would complain.

His eye fell on the bottle of Vittel.

"Ah!" said Bingo. "Darling!"

"Yes, darling?"

"Watch, darling," said Bingo. "I place the bottle so. Then, maintaining a perfect equilibrium . . ."

BINGO AND THE PEKE CRISIS

BINGO AND THE PEKE CRISIS

A BEAN was showing his sore leg to some Eggs and Piefaces in the smoking-room of the Drones Club, when a Crumpet came in. Having paused at the bar to order an Annie's Night Out, he made his way to the group.

"What," he asked, "is the trouble?"

It was a twice—or even more than that—told tale, but the Bean embarked upon it without hesitation.

"That ass Bingo Little. Called upon me at my residence the day before yesterday with a ravening Pekinese, and tried to land me with it."

"Said he had brought it as a birthday present," added one of the Eggs.

"That was his story," assented the Bean. "It doesn't hold water for an instant. It was not my birthday. And if it had been, he should have been well enough acquainted with my psychology to know that I wouldn't want a blasted, man-eating Peke with teeth like needles and a disposition that led it to take offence at the merest trifle. Scarcely had I started to direct the animal to the door, when it turned like a flash and nipped me in the calf. And if I hadn't had the presence of mind to leap on to a table, the

outcome might have been even more serious. Look!"
said the Bean. "A nasty flesh wound."

The Crumpet patted his shoulder and, giving as
his reason the fact that he was shortly about to lunch,
asked the other to redrape the limb.

"I don't wonder that the episode has left you in
something of a twitter," he said. "But I am in a
position to give you a full explanation. I saw Bingo
last night, and he has told me all. And when you
have heard the story, you will, I feel sure, agree with
me that he is more to be pitied than censured. *Tout
comprendre*," said the Crumpet, who had taken French
at school, "*c'est tout pardonner*."

You are all, he proceeded, more or less familiar
with Bingo's circumstances, and I imagine that you
regard him as one of those rare birds who are absolutely
on velvet. He eats well, sleeps well and is happily
married to a charming girl well provided with the
stuff—Rosie M. Banks, the popular female novelist,
to wit—and life for him, you feel, must be one grand,
sweet song.

But it seems to be the rule in this world that though
you may have goose, it is never pure goose. In the
most apparently Grade A ointment there is always a
fly. In Bingo's case it is the fact that he seldom, if
ever, has in his possession more than the merest
cigarette money. Mrs. Bingo seems to feel that it
is best that this should be so. She is aware of his
fondness for backing horses which, if they finish at
all, come in modestly at the tail of the procession,

and she deprecates it. A delightful girl—one of the best, and the tree, as you might say, on which the fruit of Bingo's life hangs—she is deficient in sporting blood.

So on the morning on which this story begins it was in rather sombre mood that he seated himself at the breakfast-table and speared a couple of eggs and a rasher of ham. Mrs. Bingo's six Pekes frolicked about his chair, but he ignored their civilities. He was thinking how bitter it was that he should have an absolute snip for the two o'clock at Hurst Park that afternoon and no means of cashing in on it. For his bookie, a man who seemed never to have heard of the words "Service and Co-operation," had informed him some time back that he was no longer prepared to accept mere charm of manner as a substitute for money down in advance.

He had a shot, of course, at bracing the little woman for a trifle, but without any real hope of accomplishing anything constructive. He is a chap who knows when he is chasing rainbows.

"I suppose, my dear old in-sickness-and-in-health-er," he began diffidently, "you wouldn't care for me to make a little cash for jam to-day?"

"How do you mean?" said Mrs. Bingo, who was opening letters behind the coffee apparatus.

"Well, it's like this. There's a horse——"

"Now, precious, you know I don't like you to bet."

"I would hardly call this betting. Just reaching out and gathering in the stuff, is more the way I would describe it. This horse, you see, is called Pimpled Charlie——"

"What an odd name."

"Most peculiar. And when I tell you that last night I dreamed that I was rowing in a boat on the fountain in Trafalgar Square with Oofy Prosser, you will see its extraordinary significance."

"Why?"

"Oofy's name," said Bingo in a low, grave voice, "is Alexander Charles, and what we were talking about in the boat was whether he ought not to present his collection of pimples to the nation."

Mrs. Bingo laughed a silvery laugh.

"You *are* silly!" she said indulgently, and Bingo knew that hope, never robust, must now be considered dead. If this was the attitude she proposed to take towards what practically amounted to a divine revelation, there was little to be gained by pursuing the subject. He cheesed it, accordingly, and the conversation turned to the prospects of Mrs. Bingo having a fine day for her journey. For this morning she was beetling off to Bognor Regis to spend a couple of weeks with her mother.

And he had just returned to his meditations after dealing with this topic, when he was jerked out of them by a squeal of ecstasy from behind the coffee-pot, so piercing in its timbre that it dislodged half an egg from his fork. He looked up and saw that Mrs. Bingo was brandishing a letter, beaming the while like billy-o.

"Oh, sweetie-pie," she cried, for it is in this fashion that she too often addresses him, "I've heard from Mr. Purkiss!"

"This Purkiss being who?"

"You've never met him. He's an old friend of mine. He lives quite near here. He owns a children's magazine called *Wee Tots*."

"So what?" said Bingo, still about six parasangs from getting the gist.

"I didn't like to tell you before, darling, for fear it might not come to anything, but some time ago he happened to mention to me that he was looking out for a new editor for *Wee Tots*, and I asked him to try you. I told him you had had no experience, of course, but I said you were awfully clever, and he would be there to guide you, and so on. Well, he said he would think it over, but that his present idea was to make a nephew of his the editor. But now I've had this letter from him, saying that the nephew has been county-courted by his tailor, and this has made Mr. Purkiss think his nature is too frivolous, and he wants to see you and have a talk. Oh, Bingo, I'm sure he means to give you the job."

Bingo had to sit for a moment to let all this sink in. Then he rose and kissed Mrs. Bingo tenderly.

"My little helpmeet!" he said.

He was extraordinarily bucked. The appointment, he presumed, carried with it something in the nature of a regular salary, and a regular salary was what he had been wanting for years. Judiciously laid out on those tips from above which he so frequently got in the night watches, he felt, such a stipend could speedily be built up into a vast fortune. And, even apart from the sordid angle, the idea of being an editor, with all an editor's unexampled opportunities for putting on dog and throwing his weight about, enchanted him. He looked forward with a bright enthusiasm to getting fellow-members of the Drones to send in contributions to the Kiddies' Korner, and then bunging them back as not quite up to his standard.

"He has been staying with his wife with an aunt at Tunbridge Wells, and he is coming back this morning, and he wants you to meet him under the clock at Charing Cross at twelve. Can you be there?"

"I can," said Bingo. "And not only there, but there with my hair in a braid."

"You will be able to recognize him, he says, because he will be wearing a grey tweed suit and a Homburg hat."

"I," said Bingo, with a touch of superiority, "shall be in a morning coat and the old topper."

Once again he kissed Mrs. Bingo, even more tenderly than before. And pretty soon after that it was time for her to climb aboard the car which was to take her to Bognor Regis. He saw her off at the front door, and there were unshed tears in her eyes as she made her farewells. For the poignancy of departure was intensified by the fact that, her mother's house being liberally staffed with cats, she was leaving the six Pekes behind her.

"Take care of them while I'm away," she murmured brokenly, as the animals barged into the car and got shot out again by Bagshaw, the butler. "You will look after them, won't you, darling?"

"Like a father," said Bingo. "Their welfare shall be my constant concern."

And he spoke sincerely. He liked those Pekes. His relations with them had always been based on a mutual affection and esteem. They licked his face, he scratched their stomachs. Pleasant give and take, each working for each.

"Don't forget to give them their coffee-sugar every night."

"Trust me," said Bingo, "to the death."

"And call in at Boddington and Biggs's for Ping-Poo's harness. They are mending it. Oh, and by the way," said Mrs. Bingo, opening her bag and producing currency, "when you go to Boddington and Biggs, will you pay their bill. It will save me writing out a cheque."

She slipped him a couple of fivers, embraced him fondly and drove off, leaving him waving on the front steps.

I mention this fact of his waving particularly, because it has so important a bearing on what followed. You cannot wave a hand with a couple of fivers in it without them crackling. And a couple of fivers cannot crackle in the hand of a man who has received direct information from an authoritative source that a seven-to-one shot is going to win the two o'clock race at Hurst Park without starting in his mind a certain train of thought. The car was scarcely out of sight before the Serpent had raised its head in this Garden of Eden—the Little home was one of those houses that stand in spacious grounds along the edge of Wimbledon Common—and was whispering in Bingo's ear: "How about it, old top?"

D

Now at ordinary times and in normal circumstances, Bingo is, of course, the soul of honesty and would never dream of diverting a Bond Street firm's legitimate earnings into more private and personal channels. But here, the Serpent pointed out, and Bingo agreed with him, was plainly a special case.

There could be no question, argued the Serpent, of doing down Boddington and Biggs. That could be dismissed right away. All it meant, if Bingo deposited these fivers with his bookie, to go on Pimpled Charlie's nose for the two o'clock, was that Boddington and his boy-friend would collect to-morrow instead of to-day. For if by some inconceivable chance Pimpled Charlie failed to click, all he, Bingo, had to do was to ask for a small advance on his salary from Mr. Purkiss, who by that time would have become his employer. Probably, said the Serpent, Purkiss would himself suggest some such arrangement. He pointed out to Bingo that it was not likely that he would have much difficulty in fascinating the man. Quite apart from the morning coat and the sponge-bag trousers, that topper of his was bound to exercise a spell. Once let Purkiss get a glimpse of it, and there would be very little sales-resistance from him. The thing, in short, was as good as in the bag.

It was with the lightest of hearts, accordingly, that Bingo proceeded to London an hour later, lodged the necessary with his bookie, whose office was in Oxford Street, and sauntered along to Charing Cross Station, arriving under the clock as its hands pointed to five minutes to twelve. And promptly at the hour a stout, elderly man in a grey tweed suit and a Homburg hat rolled up.

The following conversation then took place.

"Mr. Little?"

"How do you do?"

"How do you do? Lovely day."

"Beautiful."

"You are punctual, Mr. Little."

"I always am."

"A very admirable trait."

"What ho!"

And it was at this moment, just as everything was going as smooth as syrup and Bingo could see the awe and admiration burgeoning in his companion's eyes as they glued themselves on the topper, that out of the refreshment-room, wiping froth from his lips, came B. B. Tucker, Gents' Hosier and Bespoke Shirt Maker, of Bedford Street, Strand, to whom for perhaps a year and a quarter Bingo had owed three pounds, eleven and fourpence for goods supplied.

It just shows you how mental exhilaration can destroy a man's clear, cool judgment. When this idea of meeting under the clock at Charing Cross had been mooted, Bingo, all above himself at the idea of becoming editor of a powerful organ for the chicks, had forgotten prudence and right-hoed without a second thought. It was only now that he realized what madness it had been to allow himself to be lured within a mile of Charing Cross. The locality was literally stiff with shops where in his bachelor days he had run up little accounts, and you never knew when the proprietors of these shops were not going to take it into their heads, as B. B. Tucker had plainly done, to step round to the station refreshment-room for a quick one.

He was appalled. He knew how lacking in tact and *savoir-faire* men like B. B. Tucker are. When they see an old patron chatting with a friend, they do not just nod and smile and pass by. They come right up and start talking about how a settlement would oblige, and all that sort of rot. And if Purkiss was the sort of person who shrank in horror from nephews who got county-courted by their tailors, two minutes of B. B. Tucker, Bingo felt, would undo the whole effect of the topper.

And the next moment, just as Bingo had anticipated, up he came.

"Oh, Mr. Little," he began.

It was a moment for the swiftest action. There was a porter's truck behind Bingo, and most people would have resigned themselves to the fact that retreat was cut off. But Bingo was made of sterner stuff.

"Well, good-bye, Purkiss," he said, and, springing lightly over the truck, was gone with the wind. Setting a course for the main entrance, he passed out of the station at a good rate of speed and was presently in the Embankment gardens. There he remained until he considered that B. B. Tucker had had time to blow over, after which he returned to the old spot under the clock, in order to resume his conference with Purkiss at the point where it had been broken off.

Well, in one respect, everything was fine, because

B. B. Tucker had disappeared.   But in another respect the posish was not so good.   Purkiss also had legged it. He had vanished like snow off a mountain-top, and after pacing up and down for half an hour Bingo was forced to the conclusion that he wasn't coming back.   Purkiss had called it a day.   And in what frame of mind, Bingo asked himself, had he called it a day?   Now that he had leisure to think, he remembered that as he had hurdled the truck he had seen the man shoot an odd glance at him, and it occurred to him that Purkiss might have gone off thinking him a bit eccentric.   He feared the worst.   An aspirant to an editorial chair, he knew, does not win to success by jumping over trucks in the presence of his prospective proprietor.

Moodily, he went off and had a spot of lunch, and he was just getting outside his coffee when the result of the two o'clock came through on the tape.   Pimpled Charlie had failed to finish in the first three.   Providence, in other words, when urging him to put his chemise on the animal, had been pulling his leg.   It was not the first time that this had happened.

And by the afternoon post next day there arrived a letter from Purkiss which proved that his intuition had not deceived him.   He read it, and tore it into a hundred pieces.   Or so he says.   Eight, more likely.   For it was the raspberry.   Purkiss, wrote Purkiss, had given the matter his consideration and had decided to make other arrangements with regard to the editorship of *Wee Tots*.

To say that Bingo was distrait as he dined that night

would not be to overstate the facts. There was, he could see, a lot which he was going to find it difficult to explain to Mrs. Bingo on her return, and it was not, moreover, going to be any too dashed good when he had explained it. She would not be pleased about the ten quid. That alone would cast a cloud upon the home. Add the revelation that he had mucked up his chance of becoming Ye Ed., and you might say that the home would be more or less in the melting-pot.

And so, as I say, he was distrait. The six Pekes accompanied him into the library and sat waiting for their coffee-sugar, but he was too preoccupied to do the square thing by the dumb chums. His whole intellect was riveted on the problem of how to act for the best.

And then—gradually—he didn't know what first put the idea into his head—it began to steal over Bingo that there was something peculiar about these six Pekes.

It was not their appearance or behaviour. They looked the same as usual, and they behaved the same as usual. It was something subtler than that. And then, suddenly, like a wallop on the base of the skull, it came to him.

There were only five of them.

Now, to the lay mind, the fact that in a house containing six Pekes only five had rolled up at coffee-sugar-time would not have seemed so frightfully sinister. The other one is off somewhere about its domestic duties, the lay mind would have said—burying a bone, taking a refreshing nap, or something of the sort. But Bingo knew Pekes. Their psychology was an open book to him. And he was aware that if only five of them had clustered round when there was coffee-sugar going, there could be only five on the strength. The sixth must be A.W.O.L.

He had been stirring his coffee when he made the discovery, and the spoon fell from his nerveless fingers. He gazed at the Shape Of Things To Come, all of a doodah.

This was the top. He could see that. Everything else was by comparison trifling, even the trousering of Boddington and Biggs's ten quid. Mrs. Bingo loved these Pekes. She had left them with him as a sacred charge. And at the thought of what would ensue when the time came for him to give an account of his stewardship and he had to confess that he was in the red, imagination boggled. There would be tears . . . reproaches . . . oh-how-could-you's . . . Why, dash it, felt Bingo with a sudden start that nearly jerked his eyeballs out of their sockets, it was quite possible that, taking a line through that unfortunate ten quid business, she might even go so far as to suppose that he had snitched the missing animal and sold it for gold.

Shuddering strongly, he leaped from his chair and rang the bell. He wished to confer with Bagshaw and learn if by any chance the absentee was down in the kitchen. But Bagshaw was out for the evening. A parlourmaid answered the bell, and when she had informed him that the downstairs premises were entirely free from Pekes, Bingo uttered a hollow groan, grabbed his hat and started out for a walk on Wimbledon Common. There was just a faint chance—call it a hundred to eight—that the little blighter might have heard the call of the wild and was fooling about somewhere out in the great open spaces.

How long he wandered, peering about him and uttering chirruping noises, he could not have said, but it was a goodish time, and his rambles took him far afield. He had halted for a moment in quite unfamiliar territory to light a cigarette, and was about to give up the search and totter home, when suddenly he stiffened in every limb and stood goggling, the cigarette frozen on his lips.

For there, just ahead of him in the gathering dusk, he had perceived a bloke of butlerine aspect. And this butler, if butler he was, was leading on a leash a Peke so identical with Mrs. Bingo's gang that it could have been signed up with the troupe without exciting any suspicions whatever. Pekes, as you are probably aware, are either beige and hairy or chestnut and hairy. Mrs. Bingo's were chestnut and hairy.

The sight brought new life to Bingo. His razor-like intelligence had been telling him for some time that the only possible solution of the impasse was to acquire another Peke and add it to the strength, and the snag about that was, of course, that Pekes cost money—and of money at the moment he possessed but six shillings and a little bronze.

His first impulse was to leap upon this butler and choke the animal out of him with his bare hands. Wiser counsels, however, prevailed, and he contented himself with trailing the man like one of those fellows you read about who do not let a single twig snap beneath their feet. And presently the chap left the Common and turned into a quiet sort of road and finished up by going through a gate into the garden of a sizable house. And Bingo, humming nonchalantly, walked on past it till he came to some shops. He was looking for a grocer's, and eventually he found one and, going in, invested a portion of his little capital in a piece of cheese, instructing the man behind the counter to give him the ripest and breeziest he had in stock.

For Bingo, as I said before, knew Pekes, and he was aware that, while they like chicken, are fond of suet pudding and seldom pass a piece of milk chocolate if it comes their way, what they will follow to the ends of the earth and sell their souls for is cheese. And it was his intention to conceal himself in the garden till the moment of the animal's nightly airing, and then come out and make a dicker with it by means of the slab which he had just purchased.

Ten minutes later, accordingly, he was squatting in a bush, waiting for zero hour.

It is not a vigil to which he cares to look back. The experience of sitting in a bush in a strange garden, unable to smoke and with no company but your thoughts and a niffy piece of cheese, is a testing one. Ants crawled up his legs, beetles tried to muscle in between his collar and his neck, and others of God's creatures, taking advantage of the fact that he had lost his hat, got in his hair. But eventually his resolution was rewarded. A French window was thrown open, and the Peke came trotting out into the pool of light from the lamps within, followed by a stout, elderly man. And conceive Bingo's emotion when he recognized in this stout, elderly exhibit none other than old Pop Purkiss.

The sight of him was like a tonic.   Until this moment
Bingo had not been altogether free from those things of
Conscience . . . not psalms . . . yes, qualms.   He had
had qualms about the lay-out.   From time to time there
crept over him a certain commiseration for the bloke
whose household pet he was about to swipe.   A bit
tough on the poor bounder, he had felt.   These qualms
now vanished.   After the way he had let him down,
Purkiss had forfeited all claim to pity.   He was a man
who deserved to be stripped of every Peke in his
possession.

The question, however, that exercised Bingo a bit at
this juncture was how was this stripping to be done.   If
it was the man's intention to follow hard on the animal's
heels till closing time, it was difficult to see how he was
to be de-Peked without detection.

But his luck was in.   Purkiss had apparently been
entertaining himself with a spot of music on the radio,
for when he emerged it was playing a gay rumba.   And
now, as radios do, it suddenly broke off in the middle,
gave a sort of squawk and began to talk German.   And
Purkiss turned back to fiddle with it.

It gave Bingo just the time he needed.   He was out
of the bush in a jiffy, like a leopard bounding from its
lair.   There was one anxious moment when the Peke
drew back with raised eyebrows and a good deal of that
To-what-am-I-indebted-for-this-visit stuff, but for-
tunately the scent of the cheese floated to its nostrils
before it could utter more than a *sotto voce* whoofle, and
from then on everything went with a swing.   Half a
minute later, Bingo was tooling along the road with the

Peke in his arms. And eventually he reached the
Common, struck a spot which he recognized and
pushed home.

Mrs. Bingo's Pekes were all in bed when he got there,
and when he went and sprang the little stranger on
them he was delighted with the ready affability with
which they made him one of themselves. Too often,
when you introduce a ringer into a gaggle of Pekes,
there ensues a scrap like New Year's Eve in Madrid; but
to-night, after a certain amount of tentative sniffing, the
home team issued their O.K., and he left them all
curled up in their baskets like so many members of the
Athenæum. He then went off to the library, and rang
the bell. He wished, if Bagshaw had returned, to take
up with him the matter of a stiff whisky and soda.

Bagshaw had returned, all right. He appeared,
looking much refreshed from his evening out, and biffed
off and fetched the fixings. And it was as he was
preparing to depart that he said:

"Oh, about the little dog, sir."

Bingo gave a jump that nearly upset his snifter.

"Dog?" he said, in his emotion putting in about five
d's at the beginning of the word. "What dog?" he
said, inserting about seven w's in the "what."

"Little Wing-Fu, sir. I was unable to inform you
earlier, as you were not in the house when Mrs. Little's
message arrived. Mrs. Little telephoned shortly after
luncheon, instructing me to send Wing-Fu by rail to
Bognor Regis Station. It appears that there is an
artist gentleman residing in the vicinity who paints
animals' portraits, and Mrs. Little wished to have

Wing-Fu's likeness done.   I dispatched the little fellow
in a hamper, and on my return to the house found a
telegram announcing his safe arrival.   It occurred to
me that I had better mention the matter to you, as it
might have caused you some anxiety, had you chanced
to notice that one of the dogs was missing.   Good
night, sir," said Bagshaw, and popped off.

He left Bingo, as you may well suppose, chafing quite
a goodish deal.   Thanks to Mrs. Bingo's lack of a sense
of what was fitting having led her to conduct these
operations through an underling instead of approaching
him, Bingo, in her absence the head of the house, he had
imperilled his social standing by becoming a dog-
stealer.   And all for nothing.

Remembering the agonies he had gone through in
that bush—not only spiritual because of the qualms of
conscience, but physical because of the ants, the beetles
and the unidentified fauna which had got in his hair,
you can't blame him for being pretty sick about the
whole thing.   He had a sense of grievance.   Why, he
asked, had he not been informed of what was going on?
Was he a cipher?   And, anyway, where was the sense
of pandering to Wing-Fu's vanity by having his portrait
painted?   He was quite sidey enough already.

And the worst of it was that though he could see that
everything now pointed to some swift, statesmanlike
move on his part, he was dashed if he could think of one.
It was in a pretty dark mood that he swallowed a second
snort and trudged up to bed.

But there's nothing like sleeping on a thing.   He got
the solution in his bath next morning.   He saw that it

was all really quite simple. All he had to do was to take Purkiss's Peke back to the Purkiss shack, slip it in through the garden gate, and there he would be, quit of the whole unpleasant affair.

And it was only when towelling himself after the tub that he suddenly realized that he didn't know the name of Purkiss's house—not even the name of the road it was in—and that he had tacked to and fro so assiduously on his return journey that he couldn't possibly find his way back to it.

And, what was worse, for it dished the idea of looking him up in the telephone book, he couldn't remember Purkiss's name.

Oh, yes, he knows it now, all right. It is graven on his heart. If you stopped him on the street to-day and said, "Oh, by the way, Bingo, what is the name of the old blister who owns *Wee Tots*?" he would reply like a flash: "Henry Cuthbert Purkiss." But at that moment it had clean gone. You know how it is with names. Well, when I tell you that during breakfast he was convinced that it was Winterbottom and that by lunch-time he had switched to Benjafield, you will see how far the evil had spread.

And, as you will recall, his only documentary evidence no longer existed. With a peevishness which he now regretted, he had torn the fellow's letter into a hundred pieces. Or at least eight.

At this juncture, Bingo Little was a broken man.

Stripping the thing starkly down to its bare bones, he saw that the scenario was as follows. Mrs. Bingo was a woman with six Pekes. When she returned from

Bognor Regis, she would be a woman with seven Pekes. And his knowledge of human nature told him that the first thing a six-Peke woman does, on discovering that she has suddenly become a seven-Peke woman, is to ask questions. And to these questions what would be his answer?

It would, he was convinced, be perfectly useless for him to try to pretend that the extra incumbent was one which he had bought her as a surprise during her absence. Mrs. Bingo was no fool. She knew that he was not a man who frittered away his slender means buying people Pekes. She would consider the story thin. She would institute inquiries. And those inquiries must in the end lead her infallibly to this Winterbottom, or Benjafield, or whatever his name was.

It seemed to Bingo that there was only one course open to him. He must find the stowaway a comfortable home elsewhere, completely out of the Benjafield-Winterbottom zone, and he must do it immediately.

So now you understand why the poor old bird called upon you that day with the animal. And, as I said, you will probably agree that he was more to be p. than c. In this connection, he has authorized me to say that he is prepared to foot all bills for sticking-plaster, arnica, the Pasteur treatment and what not.

After your refusal to hold the baby, he appears to have lost heart. I gather that the scene was a painful one, and he did not feel like repeating it. Returning home, he decided that there was nothing to be done but somehow to dig up that name. So shortly after lunch he summoned Bagshaw to his presence.

"Bagshaw," he said, "mention some names."

"Names, sir?"

"Yes. You know. Like people have. I am trying to remember a man's name, and it eludes me. I have an idea," said Bingo, who had now begun to veer towards Jellaby, "that it begins with a J."

Bagshaw mused.

" J, sir?"

"Yes."

"Smith?" said the ass.

"Not Smith," said Bingo. "And if you mean Jones, it's not as common as that. Rather a bit on the exotic side it struck me as, when I heard it. As it might be Jerningham or Jorkins. However, in supposing that it begins with a J, I may quite easily be mistaken. Try the A's."

"Adams, sir? Allen? Ackworth? Anderson? Arkwright? Aarons? Abercrombie?"

"Switch to the B's."

"Bates? Bulstrode? Burgess? Bellinger? Biggs? Bultitude?"

"Now do me a few C's."

"Collins? Clegg? Clutterbuck? Carthew? Curley? Cabot? Cade? Cackett? Cahill? Caffrey? Cahn? Cain? Caird? Cannon? Carter? Casey? Cooley? Cuthbertson? Cope? Cork? Crowe? Cramp? Croft? Crewe? . . ."

A throbbing about the temples told Bingo that in his enfeebled state he had had about enough of this. He was just waving a hand to indicate this, when the butler, carried along by his momentum, added:

"Cruickshank? Chalmers? Cutmore? Carpenter? Cheffins? Carr? Cartwright? Cadwallader?"

And something seemed to go off in Bingo's brain like a spring.

"Cadwallader!"

"Is that the gentleman's name, sir?"

"No," said Bingo. "But it'll do."

He had suddenly recalled that Cadwallader was the name of the grocer from whom he had purchased the cheese. Starting from that grocer's door, he was pretty sure that he could find his way to Chez Purkiss. His position was clear. Cadwallader ho! was the watchword.

The prudent thing, of course, would have been to postpone the expedition until darkness had fallen, for it is under cover of night that these delicate operations are best performed. But at this season of the year, what with summertime and all that, darkness fell so dashed late, and he was all keyed up for rapid action. Refreshing his memory with another look at Cadwallader's address in the telephone book, he set out in the cool of the evening, hope in his heart and the Peke under his arm. And presently he found himself on familiar ground. Here was Cadwallader's grocery establishment, there was the road down which he had sauntered, and there a few moments later was the box hedge that fringed the Purkiss's domain and the gate through which he had entered.

He opened the gate, shoved the Peke in, bade it a brief farewell and legged it. And so home, arriving there shortly before six.

As he passed into the Little domain, he was feeling in some respects like a murderer who has at last succeeded in getting rid of the body and in other respects like Shadrach, Meshach and Abednego on emerging from the burning fiery furnace. It was as if a great load had been lifted from him. Once, he tells me, in the days of his boyhood, while enjoying a game of football at school, he was compelled in pursuance of his duties to fall on the ball and immediately afterwards became the base of a sort of pyramid consisting of himself and eight beefy members of the opposing team with sharp elbows and cleated boots. Even after all these years, he says, he can still recall the sense of buoyancy and relief when this mass of humanity eventually removed itself from the small of his back. He was feeling exactly the same relief and buoyancy now. I don't know if he actually sang, but I shouldn't be at all surprised if he didn't attempt a roundelay or two.

Bingo, like Jonah, is one of those fellows who always come up smiling. You may crush him to earth, but he will rise again. Resilient is, I believe, the word. And he now found the future, if not actually bright, at least beginning to look for the first time more or less fit for human consumption. Mistily, but growing every moment more solid, there had begun to shape itself in his mind a story which might cover that business of the Boddington and Biggs ten quid. The details wanted a bit of polishing, but the broad, basic structure was there. As for the episode at Charing Cross Station, there he proposed to stick to stout denial. It might or might not get by. It was at least worth trying.

And, in any event, he was now straight on the Peke situation.

Walking on the tips of his toes with his hat on the side of his head, Bingo drew near to the house. And it was at this point that something brushed against his leg with a cheery gurgle and, looking down, he saw that it was the Peke. Having conceived a warm regard for Bingo, and taking advantage of the fact that he had omitted to close the Purkiss's gate, it had decided to toddle along with him.

And while Bingo stood rooted to the spot, staring wanly at the adhesive animal, along came Bagshaw.

"Might I inquire, sir," said Bagshaw, "if you happen to know the telephone number of the house at which Mrs. Little is temporarily residing?"

"Why?" asked Bingo, absently, his gaze still gummed to the Peke.

"Mrs. Little's friend, Mr. Purkiss, called a short while back, desirous of obtaining information. He was anxious to telephone to Mrs. Little."

The wanness with which Bingo had been staring at the Peke was as nothing compared to the wanness with which he now stared at the butler. With the mention of that name, memory had returned to him, sweeping away all the Jellabys and Winterbottoms which had been clogging up his thought processes.

"Purkiss?" he cried, tottering on his base. "Did you say Purkiss?"

"Yes, sir."

"He has been calling here?"

"Yes, sir."

"He wanted to telephone to Mrs. Little?"

"Yes, sir."

"Did he . . . did Mr. Purkiss . . . Had he . . . Had Mr. Purkiss . . . Did Mr. Purkiss convey the impression of having something on his mind?"

"Yes, sir."

"He appeared agitated?"

"Yes, sir."

"You gathered . . . you inferred that he had some urgent communication to make to Mrs. Little?"

"Yes, sir."

Bingo drew a deep breath.

"Bagshaw," he said, "bring me a whisky and soda. A large whisky and soda. One with not too much soda in it, but with the whisky stressed. In fact, practically leave the soda out altogether."

He needed the restorative badly, and when it came lost no time in introducing it into his system. The more he contemplated Purkiss's call, the more darkly sinister did it seem to him.

Purkiss had wanted to telephone to Mrs. Bingo. He had appeared agitated. Facts like these were capable of but one interpretation. Bingo remembered the hat which he had left somewhere in the bush. Obviously, Purkiss must have found that hat, observed the initials in its band, leaped to the truth and was now trying to get hold of Mrs. Bingo to pour the whole story into her receptive ear.

There was only one thing to be done. Bingo shrank from doing it, but he could see that he had no other alternative. He must seek Purkiss out, explain all the circumstances and throw himself on his mercy, begging him as a sportsman and a gentleman to keep the whole thing under his hat. And what was worrying him was a grave doubt as to whether Purkiss was a sportsman and a gentleman. He had not much liked the man's looks on the occasion of their only meeting. It seemed to him, recalling that meeting, that Purkiss had had the appearance of an austere sort of bird, with that cold, distant look in his eyes which he, Bingo, had so often seen in those of his bookie when he was trying to get him to let the settlement stand over till a week from Wednesday.

However, the thing had to be done, and he set forth to do it. He made his way to the Purkiss's home, and the butler conducted him to the drawing-room.

"Mr. Little," he announced, and left him. And Bingo braced himself for the ordeal before him.

He could see at a glance that Purkiss was not going to be an easy audience. There was in his manner nothing of the genial host greeting the welcome popper-in. He had been standing with his back turned, looking out of the open French window, and he spun round with sickening rapidity and fixed Bingo with a frightful stare. A glare of loathing, Bingo diagnosed it as—the natural loathing of a ratepayer who sees before him the bloke who has recently lured away his Peke with cheese. And he felt that it would be necessary for him if anything in the nature of a happy ending was to be arrived at, to be winning and spellbinding as never before.

"Well?" said Purkiss.

Bingo started to make a manly clean breast of it without preamble.

"I've come about that Peke," he said.

And at that moment, before he could say another word, there barged down his windpipe, wiping speech from his lips and making him cough like the dickens, some foreign substance which might have been a fly— or a gnat—or possibly a small moth. And while he was coughing he saw Purkiss give a sort of despairing gesture.

"I was expecting this," he said.

Bingo went on coughing.

"Yes," said Purkiss, "I feared it. You are quite right. I stole the dog."

Bingo had more or less dealt with the foreign substance by this time, but he still couldn't speak. Astonishment held him dumb. Purkiss was looking like somebody in a movie caught with the goods. He was no longer glaring. There was a dull, hopeless agony in his eyes.

"You are a married man, Mr. Little," he said, "so perhaps you will understand. My wife has gone to stay with an ailing aunt at Tunbridge Wells. Shortly before she left, she bought a Pekinese dog. This she entrusted to my care, urging me on no account ever to allow it out of the house except on a lead. Last night, as the animal was merely going to step out into the garden for a few moments, I omitted the precaution. I let it run out by itself. I never saw it again."

He gulped a bit. Bingo breathed heavily a bit. He resumed.

"It was gone, and I saw that my only course was immediately to secure a substitute of similar appearance. I spent the whole of to-day going round the dog-shops of London, but without avail. And then I remembered that Mrs. Little owned several of these animals—all, as I recalled, singularly like the one I had lost. I thought she might possibly consent to sell me one of them."

He sighed somewhat.

"This evening," he went on, "I called at your house, to find that she was away and that I could not reach her by telephone. And it would be useless to write to her, for my wife returns to-morrow. So I turned away, and as I reached the gate something jumped against my leg. It was a Pekinese dog, Mr. Little, and the very image of the one I had lost. The temptation was too great . . ."

"You pinched it?" cried Bingo, shocked.

Purkiss nodded. Bingo clicked his tongue.

"A bit thick, Purkiss," he said gravely.

"I know, I know. I am fully conscious of the heinousness of what I did. My only excuse must be that I was unaware that I was being observed." He heaved another sigh. "The animal is in the kitchen," he said, "enjoying a light supper. I will ring for the butler to bring it to you. And what my wife is going to say, I shudder to think," said Purkiss, doing so.

"You fancy that she will be upset when she returns and finds no Peke to call her Mother?"

"I do, indeed."

"Then, Purkiss," said Bingo, slapping him on the shoulder, "keep this animal."

He likes to think of himself at that moment. He was sauve, kindly, full of sweetness and light. He rather imagines that Purkiss must have thought he had run up against an angel in human shape or something.

"Keep it?"

"Definitely."

"But Mrs. Little——?"

"Have no concern. My wife doesn't know from one day to another how many Pekes she's got. Just so long as there is a reasonable contingent messing about, she is satisfied. Besides," said Bingo, with quiet reproach, "she will have far too much on her mind, when she gets back, to worry about Pekes. You see, Purkiss, she had set her heart on my becoming editor of *Wee Tots*. She will be distressed when she learns of your attitude in that matter. You know what women are."

Purkiss coughed. He looked at Bingo, and quivered a bit. Then he looked at him again, and quivered a bit more. Bingo received the impression that some sort of spiritual struggle was proceeding within him.

"Do you *want* to edit *Wee Tots*, Mr. Little?" he said at length.

"I do, indeed."

"You're sure?"

"Quite sure."

"I should have thought that a young man in your position would have been too busy, too occupied——"

"Oh, no.   I could have fitted it in."

A touch of hope came into Purkiss's manner.

"The work is hard."

"No doubt I should have capable assistants."

"The salary," said Purkiss wistfully, "is not large."

"I'll tell you what," said Bingo, inspired.   "Make it larger."

Purkiss took another look, and quivered for the third time.   Then his better self triumphed.

"I shall be delighted," he said in a low voice, "if you will assume the editorship of *Wee Tots*."

Bingo patted him on the shoulder once more.

"Splendid, Purkiss," he said.   "Capital.   And now, in the matter of a small advance of salary. . . ."

THE EDITOR REGRETS

THE EDITOR REGRETS

WHEN Bingo Little's wife, the well-known female novelist Rosie M. Banks, exerted her pull and secured for Bingo the editorship of *Wee Tots*, that popular and influential organ which has done so much to mould thought in the nursery, a sort of literary renaissance swept the Drones Club. Scarcely an Egg, Bean, Pieface or Crumpet on the list of members but took pen in hand with the feeling that here was where he cashed in and got back some of the stuff that had gone down the drain at Ally Pally and Kempton Park.

It was a painful shock to the intelligentsia, accordingly, when they discovered that their old friend was not going to prove the geyser of easy money they had anticipated. In quick succession he turned down the Egg who wanted to do Racing Notes, the Bean with the inside stuff on Night Clubs, and the Pieface who suggested that he should be given a sort of roving commission to potter round the south of France and contribute gossipy articles of human interest from such centres as Cannes and Monte Carlo. Even a Crumpet who had known him since they were in sailor suits had his thoughtful piece on Some Little Known Cocktails declined with thanks.

"On the plea," said the Crumpet, "that his proprietor wouldn't like it."

"That's what he told me," said the Egg. "Who is this bally proprietor of Bingo's?"

"A man named Purkiss. It was through her lifelong friendship with Mrs. Purkiss that Mrs. Bingo was able to get Bingo the job."

"Then Purkiss can have no red blood in him," said the Egg.

"Purkiss lacks vision," said the Bean.

"Purkiss is an ass," said the Pieface.

The Crumpet shook his head.

"I'm not so sure," he said. "My belief is that Bingo merely uses Purkiss as a blind or screen. I think the man is drunk with a sense of power and definitely enjoys rejecting contributions from outside talent. And one of these days he is going to get himself into serious trouble by coming the heavy editor like this. In fact, not long ago he very nearly did so. Only the luck of the Littles saved him from taking a toss which threatened to jar his fat trouser-seat clean out of the editorial chair, never to return. I allude, of course, to the Bella Mae Jobson affair."

The Bean asked what the Bella Mae Jobson affair was, and the Crumpet, expressing surprise that he had not heard of it, said that it was the affair of Bella Mae Jobson.

"The American authoress," he explained. "Scarcely known in this country, she has for some years past been holding American childhood spellbound with her tales of Willie Walrus, Charlie Chipmunk, and other fauna. Purkiss, who had been paying a visit to New York, met her on the boat coming back, and she lent him *Charlie Chipmunk Up the Orinoco*. A single glance was enough to tell him that here was the circulation-building stuff for which *Wee Tots* had been waiting, and he entered into tentative negotiations for her whole output, asking her on arriving in London to look in at the office and fix things up with his editor—viz., Bingo.

Now, unfortunately, Purkiss's absence from the centre of things had caused Bingo to get it up his nose a bit. When on the spot, the other had a way of making criticisms and suggestions, and an editor, he tells me, feels shackled when a proprietor with bronchial catarrh keeps popping in all the time, trying to dictate the policy of the "Uncle Joe To His Chicka-biddies" page. All through these last weeks of freedom, therefore, he had been getting more and more above himself, with the result that, when informed per desk telephone that a Miss Jobson waited without he just tapped his teeth with a pencil and said: "Oh, she does, does she? Well, bung her out and tell her to write. We do not see callers without an appointment."

He then returned to the "What a Tiny Girlie Can Do to Help Mother" feature, and was still roughing it out when the door opened and in walked Purkiss, looking bronzed and fit. And after a bit of Well-here-I-am-back-again-ing and Oh-hullo-Mr.-Purkiss-did you-have-a-good-trip-ing, as is inevitable on these occasions, Purkiss said:

"By the way, Mr. Little, a Miss Jobson will be calling shortly."

Bingo gave a light laugh.

"Oh, jolly old Jobson?" he said airily. "She's been and gone, leaving not a wrack behind. I gave her the air."

"I beg your pardon?"

"Turfed her out," explained Bingo.

Purkiss reeled.

"You mean . . . you refused to see her?"

"That's right," said Bingo. "Busy. Busy, busy, busy. Much too busy to talk to females. I told her to write, stating her business legibly on one side of the paper only."

I don't know if any of you happened to see that picture, "The Hurricane," that was on not long ago. Briefly, the plot of it was that there was a bevy of unfortunate blighters on a South Sea island and the dickens of a howling tempest came along and blew them cross-eyed. I bring it up because Bingo tells me that very much the same sort of thing happened now. For some moments, he says, all he was conscious of was a vast atmospheric disturbance, with him swaying in the middle of it, and then gradually, Purkiss's remarks becoming clearer, he gathered that he had made something of a floater, and that this bird Jobson was a bird who should have been conciliated, sucked up to, given the old oil and generally made to feel that she was among friends and admirers.

"Well, I'm sorry," he said, feeling that something in the nature of an apology was indicated. "I deeply regret the whole unfortunate occurrence. I was the victim of a misunderstanding. It never crossed my mind that the above was a sweet singer specializing in chipmunks. The impression I received was of somebody trying to sell richly illustrated sets of Dumas on the easy payment plan."

Then, seeing that Purkiss had buried his face in his hands and hearing him mutter something about "God's gift to the nursery" and "ruin," he stepped across and gave him a kindly pat on the shoulder.

"Cheer up," he said. "You still have me."

"No, I haven't," said Purkiss. "You're fired."

And in words whose meaning there was no mistaking he informed Bingo that the end of the month would see his finish as Ye Ed., and that it was his, Purkiss's, dearest hope that when he, Bingo, finally left the premises, he would trip over the doormat and break his neck.

He, Purkiss, then withdrew.

His departure gave Bingo the opportunity for some intensive thinking. And as you will readily appreciate, intensive thinking was just what the situation could do with a spot of.

It was on Mrs. Bingo's reactions that he found himself brooding for the most part. There were many reasons why it cut him to the quick to be forced to relinquish his grasp on the tiller of *Wee Tots*. The salary, though small, had come under the head of manna from heaven, and the holding of the post had filled him with a spiritual pride such as he had not experienced since he won the Woolly-Mat-Tatting Prize at his first kindergarten. But what really got in amongst him was the thought of what Mrs. Bingo was going to say on hearing the news.

The Bingo *ménage*, as you are no doubt aware, is one that has been conducted from its inception on one hundred per cent Romeo and Juliet lines. She is devoted to him, and his ingrowing love for her is such that you would be justified in comparing them to a couple of turtle doves. Nevertheless, he was ill at ease. Any male turtle dove will tell you that, if conditions are right, the female turtle dove can spit on her hands and throw her weight about like Donald Duck. And it needed no diagram to show Bingo that conditions here were just right. Mrs. Bingo had taken a lot of trouble to get him this job, and when she found that through sheer fatheadedness he had chucked it away she would, something told him, have a lot of comment to make.

Little wonder, then, that the barometer of his soul pointed steadily to "Stormy." Out of the night that covered him, black as the pit from pole to pole, one solitary bit of goose presented itself—the fact that the head of the family was away at the moment, visiting friends in the country. This at least enabled him to postpone the springing of the bad tidings.

But the thought that the hour of that springing must inevitably come kept him in pretty much of a doodah, and to distract his mind he plunged into the life of pleasure. And it was at a bottle-party a couple of nights later that he found himself going like a breeze with a female of considerable attractions, and with indescribable emotion learned that her name was Jobson, Bella Mae.

It altered the whole outlook, enabling him to get an entirely new angle on the situation.

Until this moment, he had been feeling that his only chance of wangling a happy ending would be to put up a good, carefully constructed, plausible story. He had planned, accordingly, on Mrs. Bingo's return, to inform her quite frankly that he had been relieved of his portfolio for giving Purkiss's girl-friend the raspberry, and then to go on to explain why he had taken this stand. He had felt, he would say, that he owed it to her not to allow himself to be closeted with strange women. Too often, he would tell her, female visitors pat editors on the knee or even straighten their ties, and his pure soul had shrunk from the thought of anything like that happening to a sober married man like himself. It might get by, or it might not get by. It was a straight, sporting venture.

But now he saw that he could do much better than this. He could obviate all necessity for such explanations by retaining his job.

When I said that he found himself going like a breeze with this chipmunk-fancier, I used the expression in its most exact sense. I don't know if any of you have ever seen Bingo when he was going really well, but I can testify that at such times he does his stuff like a master. Irresistible charm about sums it up. Think of Ronald Colman, and you have the idea. Well, you will understand what I mean when

F

I tell you that as early as the second cocktail B. M.
Jobson was saying how lonely she felt in this big,
strange city, and he was saying "There, there" and
pointing out that this was a state of things that could
readily be adjusted. They parted in a flurry of
telephone numbers and good wishes, and he went home
feeling that the thing was in the bag.

What he proposed to do, I need scarcely explain,
was to keep after this tomato and bump up their
ripening friendship to a point where she would be able
to refuse him nothing. He would then tear off his
whiskers and reveal himself as the editor of *Wee Tots*,
whereupon she would let him have her frightful bilge
on easy terms and he would go to Purkiss and say:
"Well, Purkiss, and now how about it?" Upon
which, of course, Purkiss would immediately fold him
in a close embrace and issue a reprieve at the foot of
the scaffold.

To this end, accordingly, he devoted all his energies.
He took Bella Mae Jobson to the Zoo, the Tower of
London, Madame Tussaud's, five matinées, seven
lunches and four dinners. He also gave her a bunch
of white heather, several packets of cigarettes, eleven
lots of roses and a signed photograph. And came a
day when she said she really must buy back. She was
sailing for America on the following Wednesday, she
said, and on the Tuesday she was going to give a
lovely luncheon-party at her hotel suite and he must
be the guest of honour.

Bingo accepted effusively. The moment, he realized,
had come. He had got the thing all worked out. He

would stick on till the other guests had gone and then, while she was still mellowed with lunch, spring his big scene. He didn't see how it could miss.

It was only when a telegram arrived from Mrs. Bingo on the Monday morning, announcing that she would be returning that evening, that he began to appreciate that there might be complications which he had not foreseen.

In normal circs., the return of the wife of his b. after a longish absence would have been enough to send Bingo singing about the house. But now he didn't emit so much as a single bar, and it was with a drawn and thoughtful face that he met her at the station round about six-thirty.

"Well, well, well," he said heartily, or as heartily as he could manage, embracing her on the platform. "This is fine! This is great! This is terrific! And what a surprise, what? I thought you were planning to put in rather longer in the provinces."

Mrs. Bingo registered astonishment.

"What, miss our wedding anniversary?" she cried. She paused, and he became aware that she was eyeing him fairly narrowly. "You hadn't forgotten that to-morrow was our wedding anniversary?"

Bingo, who had given a sharp, convulsive leap like a gaffed salmon, reassembled himself.

"Me?" he cried. "I should say not. I've been ticking off the days on the calendar."

"So have I," said Mrs. Bingo. "Oh, Bingo, darling, we'll have lunch to-morrow at that little place near Charing Cross, where we had our wedding breakfast. And we'll pretend we've just been married. Won't it be fun!"

Bingo swallowed a couple of times. He was having trouble with his Adam's apple.

"Stupendous," he said.

"Only it won't be quite the same, of course, because then you hadn't an important job to hurry back to."

"No," said Bingo.

"How is everything at the office, by the way?"

"Oh, fine."

"Is Mr. Purkiss still pleased with your work?"

"Fascinated," said Bingo.

But he spoke absently, and it was with a heavy heart that he rose next morning and toyed listlessly with a fried egg and bacon. Nor was he any chirpier when he reached the editorial sanctum. He could see no daylight.

It would be possible, of course, to pop in on Bella Mae in the course of the afternoon, but he saw only too clearly that that would not be the same thing at all. The way he had had it planned out, he was to have been the life and soul of the gathering all through lunch, winning all hearts with his gay wit; and then, when the last guest had tottered away, holding his sides, and his hostess was thanking him brokenly for making her party such a success, he would have given her the works. It would be very different barging in on her at four o'clock and trying to swing the deal in cold blood.

And then, after he had been sitting for a goodish

time with his head in his hands, exercising every cell in his brain to its utmost capacity, he received an inspiration and saw what Napoleon would have done. A moment later, he was on the telephone, with Mrs. Bingo's silvery voice are-you-there-ing at the other end.

"Hullo, darling," he said.

"Hullo, angel," said Mrs. Bingo.

"Hullo, precious," said Bingo.

"Hullo, sweetie-pie," said Mrs. Bingo.

"I say, moon of my delight," said Bingo, "listen. A rather awkward thing has happened, and I should like your advice as to how to act for the best. There's a most important *literateuse* we are anxious to land for the old sheet, and the question has arisen of my taking her out to lunch to-day."

"Oh, Bingo!"

"Now, my personal inclination is to tell her to go to blazes."

"Oh, no, you mustn't do that."

"Yes, I think I will. 'Nuts to you, *literateuse*,' I shall say."

"No, Bingo, please! Of course you must take her to lunch."

"But how about our binge?"

"We can have dinner instead."

"Dinner?"

"Yes."

Bingo allowed himself to be persuaded.

"Now, that's an idea," he said. "There, I rather think, you've got something."

"Dinner will be just as good."

"Better. More suited to unbridled revelry."

"You won't have to hurry off after dinner."

"That's right."

"We'll go to a theatre and supper afterwards."

"We will, indeed," said Bingo, feeling how simple these things were, if only one used a bit of tact. "That, as I see it, is the exact programme."

"And, as a matter of fact," said Mrs. Bingo, "it's really rather convenient, because now I shall be able to go to Miss Jobson's luncheon-party, after all."

Bingo swayed like a jelly in a high wind.

"Miss who's luncheon-party?"

"Jobson. You wouldn't know her. An American writer named Bella Mae Jobson. Mrs. Purkiss rang up a little while ago, saying she was going and could I come along, because Miss Jobson has long been an admirer of my work. Of course, I refused. But now it's all right, and I shall be able to go. She sails to-morrow, so this is our last chance of meeting. Well, good-bye, my poppet, I mustn't keep you from your work any longer."

If Mrs. Bingo supposed that Bingo, having hung up the receiver, immediately returned to the task of assembling wholesome literature for the kiddies, she was gravely in error. For possibly a quarter of an hour after she had rung off, he sat motionless in his chair, using up time which Purkiss was paying him for in staring sightlessly before him and breathing in quick jerks. His whole aspect was that of a man who has unexpectedly been struck by lightning.

This, it seemed to him, was the end. He couldn't possibly roll up to the Jobson lunch, if Mrs. Bingo was going to be there. You see, in order not to divert her mind from the main issue, he had avoided informing Bella Mae that he was married. Rightly or wrongly, he had felt that better results were to be obtained by keeping this news item under his hat. And if she lugged Mrs. Bingo up to him and said, "Oh, Mr. Little, I wonder if you know Miss Rosie M. Banks?" and he replied, "Oh, rather. She's my wife," only embarrassment could ensue.

No, there was only one thing to be done. He must abandon all idea of retaining his job and go back to the plan he had originally sketched out, of explaining to Mrs. Bingo why he had refused to see Bella Mae Jobson that day when she called at the office. This, he felt with the first stirring of optimism which so far had animated him, might go pretty well after the former had met the latter. For Bella Mae, as I have said, was a female of considerable personal attractions. She had a lissome form, surmounted by a map of elfin charm and platinum blonde hair. Stranger things had happened than that Mrs. Bingo might approve his prudence in declining to be cooped up with all that sex-appeal.

Feeling somewhat better, he went out and dispatched a telegram to the Jobson, regretting his inability to be present at the festivities. And he was about to return to the office, when a sudden thought struck him amidships and he had to clutch at a passing lamp-post to keep himself from falling in his tracks.

He had remembered that signed photograph.

The whole question of signed photographs is one that bulks largely in married life. When husbands bestow them on external females, wives want to know why. And the present case was complicated by the fact that in doing the signing Bingo—with the best motives—had rather spread himself. Mere cordiality would have been bad enough, and he had gone a shade beyond the cordial. And the finished product was probably standing on the Jobson's mantelpiece and would be the first thing that Mrs. Bingo would see on entering the other's suite.

It was not an enterprise to which he in any sense of the phrase looked forward, but he saw that, if a major disaster was to be avoided and the solidity of the Bingo-Mrs. Bingo axis to be maintained, he would have to get hold of that photograph well in advance of the luncheon hour and remove it.

I don't know if you have ever called at an hotel with a view to pinching a signed photograph from one of the suites. If not, I may tell you that technical difficulties present themselves at the very outset— notably the problem of how the hell to get in. Bingo, inquiring at the desk, learned that Miss Jobson was not at home, and was for a moment encouraged by the information. It was only after he had sneaked up the stairs and was standing outside the locked door that he realized that this was not an end but a beginning. And then, just as he was feeling that he was a mere puppet in the grip of a remorseless fate and that it wasn't any use going on struggling, he saw a maid coming along the corridor, and remembered that maids have keys.

It was a moment for exerting that charm of his to the uttermost. He switched it on and allowed it to play upon the maid like a searchlight.

"Oh, hullo, maid," he said. "Good morning."

"Good morning, sir," said the maid.

"Gosh!" said Bingo. "You have a nice, kind, open, tender-hearted face. I wonder if you would do something for me. First, however," he said, shoving across a ten-bob note, "take this."

"Thank you, sir," said the maid.

"The facts, briefly," said Bingo, "are these. I am lunching to-day with Miss Jobson."

"She's out," said the maid. "I saw her go along the passage with the little dog."

"Exactly," said Bingo. "And there you have put your finger on the nub. She's out, and I want to get in. I hate waiting in hotel lobbies. You know how it is. Bores come up and tell you their troubles. Cadgers come up and try to touch you. I shall be happier in Miss Jobson's suite. Could you possibly"—here he ladled out another currency bill—"let me in?"

"Certainly, sir," said the maid, and did so.

"Thanks," said Bingo. "Heaven bless you, my dear old maid. Lovely day."

"Beautiful," said the maid.

He had scarcely crossed the threshold before he perceived that he had done the shrewd thing in sweetening her. He was a quid down, and he could ill

spare quids, but it had been worth every penny of the
money. There, as he had anticipated, was the photograph, plumb spang in the middle of the mantelpiece
where it could not have failed to catch the eye of an
incoming wife. To snatch it up and trouser it was
with him the work of a moment, and he was just
turning to the door to make the quick getaway, when
his attention was drawn to a row of bottles on the
sideboard. There they stood, smiling up at him, and
as he was feeling more than a little faint after his
ordeal he decided to have one for the road before
withdrawing.

So he sloshed some Italian vermouth into a glass,
and sloshed some French vermouth on top of it, and
was reaching for the gin, to start sloshing that, when
his heart did three double somersaults and a swan-
dive. There had come to his ears the rattle of a key
in the door.

It is difficult to say what would really have been the
right thing to do in the circumstances. Some chaps,
I suppose, would just have stayed put and tried to
pass it off with jovial breeziness. Others might have
jumped out of the window. But he wasn't feeling
equal to jovial breeziness and the suite was on the
fourth floor, so he took a middle course. He cleared
the sofa in a single bound, and had scarcely gone to
earth behind it when the door opened.

It was not Bella Mae Jobson who entered, but
his old pal the maid. She was escorting another
early popper-in. Through the gap at the bottom of
his zareba he could see the concluding portion of a

pair of trousers and a pair of boots. And when the lips above these trousers spoke, he found that this was no stranger but a familiar acquaintance. The voice was the voice of Purkiss.

"Thank you, my dear," said Purkiss.

"Thank *you*, sir," said the maid, leading Bingo to suppose that once more money had passed into her possession. He found himself brooding on the irony of the thing. Such a big day for the maid, I mean, and such a rotten one for him.

Purkiss coughed.

"I seem to be early."

"Yes, sir."

"Then, perhaps, to fill in the time, I might be taking Miss Jobson's dog for a run."

"Miss Jobson's out with the dog now, sir."

"Oh?" said Purkiss.

There was a momentary silence, and then the maid said that that was funny, and Purkiss asked what was funny.

"There ought to be another gentleman here," said the maid. "But I don't see him. Oh, yes," she proceeded, as Bingo, who for some little while now had been inhaling fluff in rather large quantities, gave a hearty sneeze, "there he is, behind the sofa."

And the next moment Bingo was aware of an eye peering down at him from the upper regions. Purkiss's eye.

"Mr. Little!" cried Purkiss.

Bingo rose, feeling that it was useless to dissemble further.

"Ah, Purkiss," he said distantly, for they were not on good terms, and with what dignity he could muster, which was not much, he rose and made for the door.

"Hey!" cried Purkiss. "Just a minute."

Bingo carried on doorwards.

"If you wish to speak to me, Purkiss," he said, "you will find me in the bar."

But it was not thither that he immediately proceeded. His need for a bracer was urgent, but even more than a bracer he wanted air. He had been under the sofa only about three minutes, but as nobody had swept there for nearly six years quite a lot of mixed substances had found their way into his lungs. He was, indeed, feeling more like a dustbin than a man. He passed through the lobby and stood outside the door of the hotel, drinking in great draughts of the life-giving, and after a while began to feel better.

The improvement in his condition, however, was purely physical. Spiritually, he continued in the depths. As he reviewed the position of affairs, his heart struck a new low. He had secured the photograph, yes, and that was good, as far as it went. But it did not, he perceived, go so dashed far. If Purkiss was to be one of the guests at the Jobson lunch, he was still waist-high in the soup and likely to sink without trace at any moment.

He could envisage just what would occur at the beano. His tortured mind threw the thing into a sort of dialogue scene.

The Apartment of B. M. Jobson. Afternoon. Discovered—B. M. Jobson and Purkiss. Enter Mrs. Bingo.

MRS. BINGO: Cheerio. I'm Rosie M. Banks.

JOBSON: Oh, what ho, Miss Banks. Do you know Mr. Purkiss?

MRS. BINGO: You betcher. He owns the paper my husband is editor of.

JOBSON: You're married, then?

MRS. BINGO: Oh, rather. Name of Little.

JOBSON: Little? Little? Odd. I know a bird named Little. In fact, when I say "know," that's understating it a bit. He's been giving me the rush of a lifetime. "Bingo," mine calls himself. Some relation, perhaps.

MRS. BINGO:

But he preferred not to sketch in Mrs. Bingo's lines. He stood there groaning in spirit. And he had just groaned for about the fifteenth time, when a car drew up before him and through a sort of mist he saw Mrs. Bingo seated at the steering-wheel.

"Oh, Bingo, darling!" cried Mrs. Bingo. "What luck finding you here. Is this where you're lunching with your writer? What an extraordinary coincidence."

It seemed to Bingo that if he was going to put up any kind of a story, now was the time to put it up. In a few brief moments Mrs. Bingo would be entering the presence of the Jobson, with results as already indicated, and her mind must be prepared.

But beyond a sort of mixed snort and gurgle he found himself unable to utter, and Mrs. Bingo carried on.

"I can't stop a minute," she said. "I've got to rush back to Mrs. Purkiss. She's in great distress. When I got to her house, to pick her up and drive her here, I found her in a terrible state. Apparently her dog has been lost. I just came here to tell Miss Jobson that we shan't be able to lunch. Will you be an angel and ring her up from the desk and explain?"

Bingo blinked. The hotel, though solidly built, seemed to be swaying above him.

"You . . . what was that you said? You won't be able to lunch with——"

"No. Mrs. Purkiss wants me with her. She's gone to bed with a hot-water bottle. So will you ring Miss Jobson up? Then I can hurry off."

Bingo drew a deep breath.

"Of course, of course, of course, of course, of course," he said. "Oh, rather. Rather. Ring Miss Jobson up . . . tell her you and Mrs. Purkiss will not be among those present . . . explain fully. A simple task. Leave it to me, light of my life."

"Thank you, darling. Good-bye."

"Good-bye," said Bingo.

She drove off, and he stood there, his eyes closed and his lips moving silently. Only once in his life before had he been conscious of this awed sense of being the favourite son of a benevolent providence. That was at his private school, when the Rev. Aubrey Upjohn, his headmaster, in the very act of raising the cane to land him a juicy one on the old spot, had ricked his shoulder and had to postpone the ceremony indefinitely.

Presently, life returned to the rigid limbs and he tottered to the bar to have one quick, followed by another rather slower. And the first person he saw there, sucking down something pink, was Purkiss. He gave him an austere look, and settled himself at the farther end of the counter. Later on, it would presumably be his nauseous task to step across and inform the man of the tragedy which had come upon his home, but the thought of holding speech with him after the way he had behaved was so revolting that he did not propose to do it until he had fortified himself with a couple of refreshers.

And he had had the first one and was waiting for the second, when he felt something pawing at his sleeve. He glanced round, and there was Purkiss with a pleading look in his eyes, like a spaniel trying to ingratiate itself with someone whom it knows to be allergic to dogs.

"Mr. Little."

"Well, Purkiss?"

"Mr. Little, it is in your power to do me a great kindness."

Well, I don't know what you would have replied to that, if you had been in Bingo's position—addressed in this fashion, I mean, by a man who had not only given you the push but in doing so had called you at least six offensive names. Personally, I would have said "Oh?" or possibly "Ho!" and that may have been what Bingo was intending to say. But before he could get going, Purkiss proceeded.

"Mr. Little, I am faced by a disaster so hideous that the mind reels, contemplating it, and only you can save me. At any moment now, my wife will be arriving here. We are lunching with Miss Jobson. Mr. Little, I appeal to you. Will you think of some suitable story and go and stand at the door and intercept her and prevent her coming to this luncheon-party? My whole future happiness depends on this."

At this juncture, Bingo's second refresher arrived and he sat sipping it thoughtfully. He could make nothing of all this, but he is a pretty intelligent chap, and he was beginning to see that circumstances had arisen which might culminate in him doing a bit of good for himself.

"It is imperative that my wife does not enter Miss Jobson's suite."

Bingo got outside the mixture, and laid the glass down.

"Tell me the whole story in your own words, Purkiss," he said.

Purkiss had produced a handkerchief, and was mopping his forehead with it. With his other hand he continued to massage Bingo's arm. His whole deportment was vastly different from what it had been when he had called Bingo those six offensive names.

"It was only late this morning," he said, "that Miss Jobson informed me on the telephone that she had invited my wife to be a guest at this luncheon-party—which, until then, I had supposed would be a *tête-à-tête* between her and myself. I may mention that I have concluded negotiations with Miss Jobson for the publication of her brilliant works. I had presumed that over the luncheon-table we would discuss such details as illustrations and general make-up."

"Matters," said Bingo coldly, "more customarily left to the editor."

"Quite, quite, but as . . . yes, quite. But the point is, Mr. Little, that in order to secure this material from Miss Jobson I had been compelled to—ah—how shall I put it——"

"Bring a little pressure to bear?"

"Precisely. Yes, it is exactly what I did. It seemed to me that the end justified the means. *Wee Tots*, as I saw it, was standing at the cross-roads. Let me secure the works of Bella Mae Jobson, and the dear old paper would soar beyond reach of competition. Let her, on the other hand, go to one of my trade rivals, and it would sustain a blow from which it might not recover. So I left no stone unturned."

"And avenues?"

"Avenues, too. I explored them all."

Bingo pursed his lips.

"I have no wish to condemn you unheard, Purkiss," he said, "but all this begins to look a bit French. Did you kiss Miss Jobson?"

A violent start shook Purkiss from stem to stern.

"No, no, no, no, no," he protested vehemently.

G

"Certainly not. Most decidedly not. Nothing of that nature whatsoever. From start to finish our relations have been conducted with the utmost circumspection on my part, complete maidenly dignity on hers. But I took her to the National Gallery, the British Museum, and a matinèe at Sadler's Wells. And then, seeing that she was weakening, I . . ."

His voice faltered and died away. Recovering it, he asked the barman for another of those pink ones for himself and whatever Bingo desired for Bingo. Then, when the tissue-restorers had appeared and he had drained his at a gulp, he found strength to continue.

"I gave her my wife's Pekinese."

"What!"

"Yes. She had admired the animal when visiting my house, and I smuggled it out in a hat-box when I left home this morning and brought it to this hotel. Ten minutes later she had signed the contract. An hour later she apparently decided to include my wife in her list of guests. Two hours after that, she was informing me of this fact on the telephone, and I hastened here in the hope of being able to purloin the animal.

"But it was not to be. She had taken it for a run. Consider my position, Mr. Little. What am I to do if my wife enters Miss Jobson's suite and finds her in possession of this dog? There will be explanations. And what will be the harvest when those explanations have been made?" He broke off, quivering in every limb. "But why are we wasting time? While we sit talking here, she may be arriving. Your post is at the door. Fly, Mr. Little!"

Bingo eyed him coldly.

"It's all very well to say 'Fly!'," he said, "but the question that springs to the lips is, 'What is there in this for me?' Really, Purkiss, after your recent behaviour I rather fail to see why I should sweat myself to the bone, lugging you out of messes. It is true," he went on meditatively, "that I have just thought of a pippin of a story which cannot fail to head Mrs. Purkiss off when she arrives, but why should I bother to dish it out? At the end of this week I cease to be in your employment. It would be a very different thing, of course, if I were continuing as editor of *Wee Tots*——"

"But you are, Mr. Little, you are."

"—at a considerably increased salary——"

"Your salary shall be doubled."

Bingo reflected.

"H'm!" he said. "And no more muscling in and trying to dictate the policy of the 'Uncle Joe To His Chickabiddies' page?"

"None, none. From now on, none. You shall have a completely free hand."

"Then, Purkiss, you may set your mind at rest. Mrs. Purkiss will not be present at the luncheon-party."

"You guarantee that?"

"I guarantee it," said Bingo. "Just step along with me to the writing-room and embody the terms of our new contract in a brief letter, and I will do the needful."

SONNY BOY

SONNY BOY

ON the question of whether Bingo Little was ethically justified in bringing his baby into the club and standing it a milk straight in the smoking-room, opinion at the Drones was sharply divided. A Bean with dark circles under his eyes said that it was not the sort of thing a chap wanted to see suddenly when he looked in for a drop of something to correct a slight queasiness after an exacting night. A more charitable Egg argued that as the child was presumably coming up for election later on, it was as well for it to get to know the members. A Pieface thought that if Bingo did let the young thug loose on the premises, he ought at least to give the committee a personal guarantee for all hats, coats and umbrellas.

"Because if ever I saw a baby that looked like something that was one jump ahead of the police," said the Pieface, "it is this baby of Bingo's. Definitely the criminal type. It reminds me of Edward G. Robinson."

A Crumpet, always well informed, was able to throw a rather interesting light on the situation.

"I agree," he said, "that Algernon Aubrey Little is not a child whom I personally would care to meet down a dark alley, but Bingo assures me that its heart is in the right place, and as for his bringing it here and lushing it up, that is readily explained. He is grateful to this baby and feels that the best is none too good for it. By doing the right thing at the right time, it recently pulled him out of a very nasty spot. It is not too much to say, he tells me, that but for its intervention a situation would have been precipitated in his home life which might well have staggered humanity."

When in the second year of his marriage to Rosie M. Banks, the eminent female novelist, his union was blessed and this bouncing boy appeared on the London scene, Bingo's reactions (said the Crumpet) were, I gather, very much the same as yours. Introduced to the child in the nursing home, he recoiled with a startled "Oi!" and as the days went by the feeling that he had run up against something red-hot in no way diminished.

The only thing that prevented a father's love from faltering was the fact that there was in his possession a photograph of himself at the same early age, in which he, too, looked like a homicidal fried egg. This proof that it was possible for a child, in spite of a rocky start, to turn eventually into a suave and polished boulevardier with finely chiselled features heartened him a good deal, causing him to hope for the best.

Meanwhile, however, there was no getting away from it that the little stranger was at the moment as pronounced a gargoyle as ever drained a bottle, and Bingo, finding that a horse of that name was running in the three o'clock at Plumpton, had no hesitation in

putting ten pounds on it to cop. Always on the look-
out for omens from on high, he thought that this must
have been what the child had been sent for.

The failure of Gargoyle to finish in the first six left
him in a position of considerable financial embarrassment. The tenner which he had placed on its nose
was the last one he had, and its loss meant that he
would have to go a month without cigarettes, cocktails,
and those other luxuries which to the man of refinement
are so much more necessary than necessities.

For there was no glittering prospect open to him of
being able to touch the head of the house for a trifle to
be going on with. Mrs. Bingo's last words, before
leaving for Worcestershire some two weeks previously
to see her mother through a course of treatment at the
Droitwich brine baths, had contained a strong injunc-
tion to him not to bet in her absence; and any attempt
on his part to palliate his action by showing that he
had supposed himself to be betting on a certainty
would, he felt, be badly received.

No, the cash, if it was to be raised, must be raised
from some other source, and in these circumstances his
thoughts, as they had so often done before, turned to
Oofy Prosser. That it was never a simple task to get
into Oofy's ribs, but one always calculated to test the
stoutest, he would have been the first to concede. But
it so happened that in the last few days the club's tame
millionaire had shown himself unexpectedly friendly.
On one occasion, going into the writing-room to dash off
a letter to his tailor which he hoped would lead to an
appeasement, Bingo had found him there, busy on

what appeared to be a poem: and Oofy, after asking
him if he knew any good rhymes to "eyes of blue," had
gone on to discuss the married state with him, giving it
as his opinion that it was the only life.

The conclusion Bingo drew was that love had at last
found Oofy Prosser, and an Oofy in love, he reasoned,
might—nay, must—be an Oofy in a melting mood
which would lead him to scatter the stuff in heaping
handfuls. It was with bright confidence, accordingly,
that he made his way to the block of flats in Park Lane
where the other has his lair, and it was with a feeling
that his luck was in that, reaching the front door, he
met Oofy coming out.

"Oh, hullo, Oofy," he said. "Good morning, Oofy.
I say, Oofy——"

I suppose years of being the official moneyed man of
the Drones have given Oofy Prosser a sort of sixth
sense. You might almost say that he is clairvoyant.
Without waiting to hear more, he now made a quick
sideways leap, like an antelope spotting a tiger, and was
off in a cab, leaving Bingo standing there considering
how to act for the best.

Taking a line through stoats and weasels, he decided
that the only thing to do was to continue doggedly on
the trail, so he toddled off to the Savoy Grill, whither
he had heard the driver being told to drive, and
arriving there some twenty minutes later found Oofy
in the lobby with a girl. It was with considerable
pleasure that he recognized in her an old pal, with
whom in his bachelor days he had frequently trodden
the measure, for this enabled him to well-well-well and

horn in. And once Bingo has horned in, he is not easy to dislodge. A few minutes later, they were all seated round a table and he was telling the wine waiter to be sure to take the chill off the claret.

It didn't occur to him at the time, but, looking back, Bingo had a feeling that Oofy would have been just as pleased if he hadn't shown up. There was a sort of constraint at the meal. Bingo was all right. He prattled freely. And the girl was all right. She prattled freely, too. It was just that Oofy seemed not quite to have got the party spirit. Silent. Distrait. Absent-minded. Inclined to fidget in his chair and drum on the tablecloth with his fingers.

After the coffee, the girl said, Well, she supposed she ought to be hareing to Charing Cross and catching her train—she, it appeared, being headed for a country house visit in Kent. Oofy, brightening a little, said he would come and see her off. And Bingo, faithful to his policy of not letting Oofy out of his sight, said he would come too. So they all tooled along, and after the train had pulled out Bingo, linking his arm in Oofy's, said:

"I say, Oofy, I wonder if you would do me a trifling favour?"

Even as he spoke, he tells me he seemed to notice something odd in his companion's manner. Oofy's eyes had a sort of bleak glazed look in them.

"Oh?" he said distantly. "You do, do you? And what is it, my bright young limpet? What can I do for you, my adhesive old porous plaster?"

"Could you lend me a tenner, Oofy, old man?"

"No, I couldn't."

"It would save my life."

"There," said Oofy, "you have put your finger on the insuperable objection to the scheme. I see no percentage in your being alive. I wish you were a corpse, preferably a mangled one. I should like to dance on your remains."

Bingo was surprised.

"Dance on my remains?"

"All over them."

Bingo drew himself up. He has his pride.

"Oh?" he said. "Well, in that case, tinkerty-tonk."

The interview then terminated. Oofy hailed a cab, and Bingo returned to his Wimbledon home. And he had not been there long when he was informed that he was wanted on the telephone. He went to the instrument and heard Oofy's voice.

"Hullo," said Oofy. "Is that you? I say, you remember me saying I would like to dance on your mangled remains?"

"I do."

"Well, I've been thinking it over——"

Bingo's austerity vanished. He saw what had happened. Shortly after they had separated, Oofy's better nature must have asserted itself, causing remorse to set in. And he was just about to tell him not to give it another thought, because we all say more than we mean in moments of heat, when Oofy continued:

"——thinking it over," he said, "and I would like to add 'in hobnailed boots.' Good-bye."

It was a tight-lipped and pensive Bingo Little who hung up the receiver and returned to the drawing-room, where he had been tucking into tea and muffins. As he resumed the meal, the tea turned to wormwood and the muffins to ashes in his mouth. The thought of having to get through a solid month without cocktails and cigarettes gashed him like a knife. And he was just wondering if it might not be best, after all, to go to the last awful extreme of confessing everything to Mrs. Bingo, when the afternoon post came in, and there was a letter from her. And out of it, as he tore open the envelope, tumbled a ten-pound note.

Bingo tells me that his emotions at this moment were almost indescribable. For quite a while, he says, he remained motionless in his chair with eyes closed, murmuring: "What a pal! What a helpmeet!" Then he opened his eyes and started to read the letter.

It was a longish letter, all about the people at the hotel and a kitten she had struck up an acquaintance with and what her mother looked like when floating in the brine bath, and so on and so forth, and it wasn't till the end that the tenner got a mention. Like all women, Mrs. Bingo kept the big stuff for her postscript.

PS. (she wrote).—I am enclosing ten pounds. I want you to go to the bank and open an account for little Algy with it. Don't you think it will be too sweet, him having his own little account and his own little wee passbook?

I suppose if a fairly sinewy mule had suddenly

kicked Bingo in the face, he might have felt a bit worse, but not much. The letter fell from his nerveless hands. Apart from the hideous shock of finding that he hadn't clicked, after all, he thoroughly disapproved of the whole project. Himself strongly in favour of sharing the wealth, it seemed to him that the last thing to place in the hands of an impressionable child was a little wee passbook, starting it off in life—as it infallibly must—with capitalistic ideas out of tune with the trend of modern enlightened thought. Slip a baby ten quid, he reasoned, and before you knew where you were you had got another Economic Royalist on your hands.

So uncompromising were his views on the subject that there was a moment when he found himself toying with the notion of writing back and telling Mrs. Bingo— in the child's best interests—that he had received a letter from her stating that she was enclosing ten pounds, but that, owing doubtless to a momentary carelessness on her part, no ten pounds had arrived with it. However, he dismissed the idea—not because it was not good, but because something told him that it was not good enough. Mrs. Bingo was a woman who wrote novels about girls who wanted to be loved for themselves alone, but she was not lacking in astuteness.

He finished his tea and muffins, and then, ordering the perambulator, had the son and heir decanted into it and started off for a saunter on Wimbledon Common. Many young fathers, I believe, shrink from this task, considering that it lowers their prestige, but Bingo had always enjoyed it.

To-day, however, the jaunt was robbed of all its

pleasures by the brooding melancholy into which the
sight of the child, lying there dumb and aloof with a
thumb in its mouth, plunged him.   Hitherto, he had
always accepted with equanimity the fact that it was
impossible for there to be any real exchange of ideas
between his offspring and himself.   An occasional
gurgle from the former, and on his side a few musical
chirrups, had served to keep them in touch.   But now
the thought that they were separated by an impassable
gulf which no chirrups could bridge, seemed to him
poignant and tragic to a degree.

Here, he reflected, was he—penniless; and there was
the infant—rolling in the stuff; and absolutely no way
of getting together and adjusting things.   If only he
could have got through to Algernon Aubrey the facts
relating to his destitute condition, he was convinced
that there would have been no difficulty about arrang-
ing a temporary loan.   It was the old story of frozen
assets, which, as everyone knows, is the devil of a
business and stifles commerce at the source.

So preoccupied was he with these moody meditations
that it was not immediately that he discovered that
somebody was speaking his name.   Then, looking up
with a start, he saw that a stout man in a frock coat and
a bowler hat had come alongside, wheeling a perambulator containing a blob-faced baby.

"Good evening, Mr. Little," he said, and Bingo saw
that it was his bookie, Charles ("Charlie Always
Pays") Pikelet, the man who had acted as party of the
second part in the recent deal over the horse Gargoyle.
Having seen him before only at race meetings—where,

doubtless from the best of motives, he affected chess-board tweeds and a white panama—he had not imme-diately recognized him.

"Why, hullo, Mr. Pikelet," he said.

He was not really feeling in the vein for conversation and would have preferred to be alone with his thoughts, but the other appeared to be desirous of chatting, and he was prepared to stretch a point to oblige him. The prudent man always endeavours to keep in with bookies.

"I didn't know you lived in these parts. Is that your baby?"

"Ah," said Charles Pikelet, speaking despondently. He gave a quick look into the interior of the perambu-lator to which he was attached, and winced like one who has seen some fearful sight.

"Kitchy-kitchy," said Bingo.

"How do you mean, kitchy-kitchy?" asked Mr. Pikelet, puzzled.

"I was speaking to the baby," explained Bingo. "A pretty child," he added, feeling that there was nothing to be lost by giving the man the old oil.

Charles Pikelet looked up, amazement in his eyes.

"Pretty?"

"Well, of course," said Bingo, his native honesty compelling him to qualify the statement, "I don't say he—if it is a he—is a Robert Taylor or—if a she—a Carole Lombard. Pretty compared with mine, I mean."

Again Charles Pikelet appeared dumbfounded.

"Are you standing there and telling me this baby of mine isn't uglier than that baby of yours?" he cried incredulously.

It was Bingo's turn to be stunned.

"Are you standing there and telling me it is?"

"I certainly am. Why, yours looks human."

Bingo could scarcely believe his ears.

"Human? Mine?"

"Well, practically human."

"My poor misguided Pikelet, you're talking rot."

"Rot, eh?" said Charles Pikelet, stung. "Perhaps you'd care to have a bet on it? Five to one I'm offering that my little Arabella here stands alone as the ugliest baby in Wimbledon."

A sudden thrill shot through Bingo. No one has a keener eye than he for recognizing money for pickles.

"Take a tenner?"

"Tenner it is."

"Okay," said Bingo.

"Kayo," said Charles Pikelet. "Where's your tenner?"

This introduction of a rather sordid note into the discussion caused Bingo to start uneasily.

"Oh, dash it," he protested, "surely elasticity of credit is the very basis of these transactions. Chalk it up on the slate."

Mr. Pikelet said he hadn't got a slate.

Bingo had to think quickly. He had a tenner on his person, of course, but he realized that it was in the nature of trust money, and he had no means of conferring with Algernon Aubrey and ascertaining whether the child would wish to slip it to him. It might be that he had inherited his mother's lack of the sporting spirit.

And then, with quick revulsion, he felt that he was

H

misjudging the little fellow.   No son of his would want
to pass up a snip like this.

"All right," he said.   "Here you are."

He produced the note, and allowed it to crackle
before Charles Pikelet's eyes.

"Right," said Charles Pikelet, satisfied.   "Here's
my fifty.   And we'll put the decision up to this
policeman that's coming along.   Hey, officer."

"Gents?" said the policeman, halting.   He was a
large, comfortable man with an honest face.   Bingo
liked the look of him, and was well content to place the
judging in his hands.

"Officer," said Charles Pikelet, "to settle a bet, is
this baby here uglier than that baby there?"

"Or vice versa?" said Bingo.

The policeman brooded over the two perambulators.

"They're neither of 'em to be compared with the one
I've got at home," he said, a little smugly.   "There's a
baby with a face that *would* stop a clock.   And the
missus thinks it's a beauty.   I've had many a hearty
laugh over that," said the policeman indulgently.

Both Charles Pikelet and Bingo felt that he was
straying from the point.

"Never mind about your baby," said Charles Pikelet.

"No," said Bingo.   "Stick closely to the *res.*"

"Your baby isn't a runner," said Charles Pikelet.
"Only the above have arrived."

Called to order, the policeman intensified his scrutiny.
He looked from the one perambulator to the other, and
then from the other perambulator to the one.   And it
suddenly came over Bingo like a cold douche that this

hesitation could mean only one thing. It was not going to be the absurdly simple walk-over which he had anticipated.

"H'm!" said the policeman.

"Ha!" said the policeman.

Bingo's heart stood still. It was now plain to him that there was to be a desperately close finish. But he tells me that he is convinced that his entry would have nosed home, had it not been for a bit of extraordinary bad luck in the straight. Just as the policeman stood vacillating, there peeped through the clouds a ray of sunshine. It fell on Arabella Pikelet's face, causing her to screw it up in a hideous grimace. And at the same instant, with the race neck and neck, she suddenly started blowing bubbles out of the corner of her mouth.

The policeman hesitated no longer. He took Miss Pikelet's hand and raised it.

"The winnah!" he said. "But you ought to see the one I've got at home."

If the muffins which Bingo had had for tea had turned to ashes in his mouth, it was as nothing compared with what happened to the chump chop and fried which he had for dinner. For by that time his numbed brain, throwing off the coma into which it had fallen, really got busy, pointing out to him the various angles of the frightful mess he had let himself into. It stripped the seven veils from the situation, and allowed him to see it in all its stark grimness.

Between Bingo and Mrs. Bingo there existed an almost perfect love. From the very inception of their union, they had been like ham and eggs. But he doubted whether the most Grade A affection could stand up against the revelation of what he had done this day. Look at his story from whatever angle you pleased, it remained one that reflected little credit on a young father and at the best must inevitably lead to "Oh, how could you's?" And the whole wheeze in married life, he had come to learn, was to give the opposite number as few opportunities of saying "Oh, how could you?" as possible.

And that story would have to be told. The first thing Mrs. Bingo would want to see on her return would be Algernon Aubrey's passbook, and from the statement that no such passbook existed to the final, stammering confession would be but a step. No wonder that as he sat musing in his chair after dinner the eyes were haggard, the face drawn and the limbs inclined to twitch.

He was just jotting down on the back of an envelope a few rough notes such as "Pocket picked," and "Took the bally thing out of my pocket on a windy morning and it blew out of my hand," and speculating on the chances of these getting by, when he was called to the telephone to take a trunk call and found Mrs. Bingo on the other end of the wire.

"Hullo," said Mrs. Bingo.

"Hullo," said Bingo.

"Oh, hullo, darling."

"Hullo, precious."

"Hullo, sweetie-pie."

"Hullo, angel."

"Are you there?" said Mrs. Bingo. "How's Algy?"

"Oh, fine."

"As beautiful as ever?"

"Substantially, yes."

"Have you got my letter?"

"Yes."

"And the ten pounds?"

"Yes."

"Don't you think it's a wonderful idea?"

"Terrific."

"I suppose it was too late to go to the bank to-day?"

"Yes."

"Well, go there to-morrow morning before you come to Paddington."

"Paddington?"

"Yes. To meet me. We're coming home to-morrow. Mother swallowed some brine this morning, and thinks she'd rather go and take the mud baths at Pistany instead."

At any moment less tense than the present one, the thought of Mrs. Bingo's mother being as far away as Pistany would have been enough to cause Bingo's spirits to soar. But now the news hardly made an impression on him. All he could think of was that the morrow would see Mrs. Bingo in his midst. And then the bitter reckoning.

"The train gets to Paddington about twelve. Mind you're there."

"I'll be there."

"And bring Algy."

"Right-ho."

"Oh, and, Bingo. Most important. You know my desk?"

"Desk. Yes."

"Look in the middle top drawer."

"Middle top drawer. Right."

"I left the proofs of my Christmas story for *Woman's Wonder* there, and I've had a very sniffy telegram saying that they must have them to-morrow morning. So will you be an angel and correct them and send them off by to-night's post without fail? You can't miss them. Middle top drawer of my desk, and the title is 'Tiny Fingers.' And now I must go back to Mother. She's still coughing. Good-bye, darling."

"Good-bye, precious."

"Good-bye, lambkin."

"Good-bye, my dream rabbit."

Bingo hung up the receiver, and made his way to the study. He found the proofs of "Tiny Fingers," and taking pencil in hand seated himself at the desk and started in on them.

His heart was heavier than ever. Normally, the news that his mother-in-law had been swallowing brine and was still coughing would have brought a sparkle to his eyes and a happy smile to his lips, but now it left him cold. He was thinking of the conversation which had just concluded and remembering how cordial Mrs. Bingo's voice had been, how cheery, how loving—so absolutely in all respects the voice of a woman who thinks her husband a king among men. How different from the flat, metallic voice which was going to say "*What!*" to him in the near future.

And then suddenly, as he brooded over the galley
slips, a sharp thrill permeated his frame and he sat up
in his chair as if a new, firm backbone had been inserted
in place of the couple of feet of spaghetti he had been
getting along with up till now. In the middle of slip
two the story had started to develop, and the way in
which it developed caused hope to dawn again.

I don't know if any of you are readers of Mrs. Bingo's
output. If not, I may inform you that she goes in
pretty wholeheartedly for the fruitily sentimental.
This is so even at ordinary times, and for a Christmas
number, of course, she naturally makes a special effort.
In "Tiny Fingers" she had chucked off the wraps
completely. Scooping up snow and holly and robin
redbreasts and carol-singing villagers in both hands,
she had let herself go and given her public the works.

Bingo, when I last saw him, told me the plot of
"Tiny Fingers" in pitiless detail, but all I need touch
on now is its main theme. It was about a hard-
hearted godfather who had given his goddaughter the
air for marrying the young artist, and they came right
back at him by shoving the baby under his nose on
Christmas Eve—the big scene, of course, being the
final one, where the old buster sits in his panelled
library, steadying the child on his knee with one hand
while writing a whacking big cheque with the other.
And the reason it made so deep an impression on Bingo
was that he had suddenly remembered that Oofy
Prosser was Algernon Aubrey's godfather. And what
he was asking himself was, if this ringing-in-the-baby
wheeze had worked with Sir Aylmer Mauleverer, the

hardest nut in the old-world village of Meadowvale, why shouldn't it work with Oofy?

It was true that the two cases were not exactly parallel, Sir Aylmer having had snow and robin redbreasts to contend against and it now being the middle of June. It was true, also, that Oofy, when guardedly consenting to hold the towel for Algernon Aubrey, had expressly stipulated that there must be no funny business and that a small silver mug was to be accepted in full settlement. Nevertheless, Bingo went to bed in optimistic mood. Indeed, his last thought before dropping off to sleep was a speculation as to whether if the baby played its cards right, it might not be possible to work Oofy up into three figures.

He had come down a bit in his budget, of course, by the time he set out for Park Lane next morning. One always does after sleeping on these things. As he saw it now, twenty quid was about what it ought to pan out at. This, however, cut fifty-fifty between principal and manager, would be ample. He was no hog. All he wanted was to place child and self on a sound financial footing, and as he reached Oofy's flat and pressed the bell, he was convinced that the thing was in the bag.

In a less sanguine frame of mind, he might have been discouraged by the fact that the infant was looking more than ever like some mass-assassin who has been blackballed by the Devil's Island Social and Outing Club as unfit to associate with the members; but his experience with Charles Pikelet and the policeman had shown him that this was how all babies of that age looked, and he had no reason to suppose that the one in "Tiny Fingers" had been any different. The only thing Mrs. Bingo had stressed about the latter had been its pink toes, and no doubt Algernon Aubrey, if called upon to do so, could swing as pink a toe as the next child. It was with bright exuberance that he addressed Oofy's man, Corker, as he opened the door.

"Oh, hullo, Corker. Lovely morning. Mr. Prosser in?"

Corker did not reply immediately. The sight of Algernon Aubrey seemed momentarily to have wiped speech from his lips. Perfectly trained valet though he was, he had started back on perceiving him, his arms raised in a rudimentary posture of self-defence.

"Yes, sir," he replied at length. "Mr. Prosser is at home. But he is not up yet, sir. He was out late last night."

Bingo nodded intelligently. Oofy's practice of going out on the tiles and returning with the morning milk was familiar to him.

"Ah, well," he said tolerantly. "Young blood, Corker, eh?"

"Yes, sir."

"It's a poor heart that never rejoices."

"So I have been informed, sir."

"I'll just pop in and pip-pip."

"Very good, sir. Shall I take your luggage?"

"Eh? Oh, no thanks. This is Mr. Prosser's godson. I want them to meet. This'll be the first time he's seen him."

"Indeed, sir?"

"Rather make his day, what?"

"So I should be disposed to imagine, sir. If you will follow me, sir. Mr. Prosser is in the sitting-room."

"In the sitting-room? I thought you said he was in bed."

"No, sir. On his return home this morning, Mr. Prosser appears to have decided not to go to bed. You will find him in the fireplace."

And so it proved. Oofy Prosser was lying with his head in the fender and his mouth open. He had on an opera hat and what would have been faultless evening dress if he had had a tie on instead of a blue ribbon of the sort which the delicately nurtured use to bind up their hair. In one hand he was clutching a pink balloon, and across his shirt front was written in lipstick the word "Whoops." His whole aspect was so plainly that of a man whom it would be unwise to stir that Bingo, chewing a thoughtful lip, stood pondering on what was the best policy to pursue.

It was a glance at his watch that decided him. He saw that he had been running rather behind schedule, and that if he was to meet Mrs. Bingo at Paddington at twelve-five he would have to be starting at once.

"This, Corker," he said to Corker, "has made things a bit complex, Corker. I've got to be at Paddington in ten minutes, and everything seems to point to the fact that Mr. Prosser, if roused abruptly, may wake up cross. Better, I think, to let him have his sleep out. So here is the procedure, as I see it. I will leave this baby on the floor beside him, so that they can get

together in due course, and I will look in and collect
it on my way back."

"Very good, sir."

"Now, Mr. Prosser's first move, on waking and
finding the place crawling with issue, will no doubt be
to ring for you and ask what it's all about. You will
then say: 'This is your godson, sir.' You couldn't
manage 'itsy-bitsy godson,' could you?"

"No, sir."

"I was afraid not. Still, you've got the idea of the
thing? Good. Fine. Right-ho."

The train from Droitwich was rolling in just as Bingo
came on to the platform, and a moment later he spotted
Mrs. Bingo getting out. She was supporting her
mother, who still seemed rocky on the pins, but on
seeing him she detached herself from the old geezer,
allowing her to navigate temporarily under her own
steam, and flung herself into his arms.

"Bingo, darling!"

"Rosie, my pre-eminent old egg!"

"Well, it is nice being back with you again. I feel
as if I had been away years. Where's Algy?"

"I left him at Oofy Prosser's. His godfather, you
know. I had a minute or two to spare on my way
here, so I looked in on Oofy. He was all over the child
and just wouldn't let him go. So I arranged that I
would call in for him on my way back."

"I see. Then I had better meet you there after I've
taken Mother to her flat. She's not at all well."

"No, I noticed she seemed to be looking a bit down

among the wines and spirits," said Bingo, casting a gratified glance at the old object, who was now propping herself up against a passing porter. "The sooner you get her off to the mud baths, the better. All right, then. See you at Oofy's."

"Where does he live?"

"Bloxham Mansions, Park Lane."

"I'll be there as soon as I can. Oh, Bingo, darling, did you deposit that money for Algy?"

Bingo struck his forehead.

"Well, I'm dashed! In the excitement of meeting you, my dream of joy, I clean forgot. We'll do it together after leaving Oofy."

Brave words, of course, but as he hiked back to Bloxham Mansions there suddenly came on him for the first time an unnerving feeling of doubt as to whether he was justified in taking it for granted that Oofy would come across. At the moment when he had conceived the scheme of using Algernon Aubrey as a softening influence, he had felt that it was a cinch. It had taken only about five minutes of his godson's society to bring the milk of human kindness sloshing out of Sir Aylmer Mauleverer in bucketfuls, and he had supposed that the same thing would happen with Oofy. But now there began to burgeon within him a chilling uncertainty, which became intensified with every step he took.

It had only just occurred to him that Algernon Aubrey was up against a much stiffer proposition than the child in "Tiny Fingers." Sir Aylmer Mauleverer had been a healthy, outdoor man, the sort that springs from bed and makes a hearty breakfast. There had been no suggestion, as far as he could remember, of him having a morning head. Oofy on the other hand, it was only too abundantly evident, was going to have when he awoke to face a new day, a morning head of the first water. Everything, he realized, turned on how that head would affect a godfather's outlook.

It was with tense anxiety that he demanded hot news from Corker as the door opened.

"Any developments, Corker?"

"Well, yes and no, sir."

"How do you mean, yes and no? Has Mr. Prosser rung?"

"No, sir."

"Then he's still asleep?"

"No, sir."

"But you said he hadn't rung."

"No, sir. But a moment ago I heard him utter a cry."

"A cry?"

"Yes, sir. A piercing cry, indicative of considerable distress of mind. It was in many respects similar to his ejaculation on the morning of January the first of the present year, on the occasion when he supposed— mistakenly—that he had seen a pink elephant."

Bingo frowned.

"I don't like that."

"Nor did Mr. Prosser, sir."

"I mean, I don't like the way things seem to have been shaping. You're a man of the world, Corker. You know as well as I do that godfathers don't utter piercing cries on meeting their godsons, unless there is something seriously amiss. I think I'll step along and take a dekko."

He did so, and, entering the sitting-room and noting contents, halted with raised eyebrows.

Algernon Aubrey was seated on the floor, his attention riveted on the balloon which he appeared to be trying to swallow. Oofy Prosser was standing on the mantelpiece, gazing down with bulging eyes. Bingo is a pretty shrewd sort of chap, and it didn't take him long to see that there was a sense of strain in the atmosphere. He thought the tactful thing to do was to pass it off as if one hadn't noticed anything.

"Hullo, Oofy," he said.

"Hullo, Bingo," said Oofy.

"Nice morning," said Bingo.

"Wonderful weather we're having," said Oofy.

They chatted for a while about the prospects for Hurst Park and the latest mid-European political developments, and then there was a pause. It was Oofy who eventually broke it.

"Tell me, Bingo," he said, speaking with a rather overdone carelessness, "I wonder if by any chance you can see anything on the floor, just over there by the fireplace. I dare say it's only my imagination, but it seems to me——"

"Do you mean the baby?"

Oofy gave a long sort of whistling gasp.

"It *is* a baby? I mean, you can see it, too?"

"Oh, rather. With the naked eye," said Bingo. "Pipsy-wipsy," he added, lugging the child into the

conversation so that it wouldn't feel out of it. "Dada
can see you."

Oofy started.

"Did you say 'dada'?"

"'Dada' was the word."

"Is this your baby?"

"That's right."

"The little blighter I gave that silver mug to?"

"None other."

"What's he doing here?"

"Oh, just paying a social call."

"Well," said Oofy, in an aggrieved voice, starting
to climb down, "if he had had the sense to explain
that at the outset, I would have been spared a terrible
experience. I came in a bit late last night and sank
into a refreshing sleep on the floor, and I woke to
find a frightful face glaring into mine. Naturally,
I thought the strain had been too much and that I
was seeing things."

"Would you care to kiss your godson?"

Oofy shuddered strongly.

"Don't say such things, even in fun," he begged.

He reached the floor, and stood staring at Algernon
Aubrey from a safe distance.

"And to think," he murmured, "that I thought of
getting married!"

"Marriage is all right," argued Bingo.

"True," Oofy conceded, "up to a certain point.
But the risk! The fearful risk! You relax your
vigilance for a second, you turn your head for a single
instant, and bing! something like that happens."

"Popsy-wopsy," said Bingo.

"It's no good saying 'popsy-wopsy'—it's appalling. Bingo," said Oofy, speaking in a low, trembling voice, "do you realize that, but for your muscling in on that lunch of mine, this might have happened to me? Yes," he went on, paling beneath his pimples, "I assure you. I was definitely planning to propose to that girl over the coffee and cigarettes. And you came along and saved me." He drew a deep breath. "Bingo, old chap, don't I seem to recall hearing you ask me for a fiver or something?"

"A tenner."

Oofy shook his head.

"It's not enough," he said. "Would you mind if I made it fifty?"

"Not a bit."

"You've no objection?"

"None whatever, old man."

"Good," said Oofy.

"Fine," said Bingo.

"Excuse me, sir," said Corker, appearing in the doorway, "the hall porter has rung up to say that Mrs. Little is waiting for Mr. Little downstairs."

"Tell her I'll be there in two ticks, with bells on," said Bingo.

ANSELM GETS HIS CHANCE

ANSELM GETS HIS CHANCE

THE Summer Sunday was drawing to a close.
Twilight had fallen on the little garden of the
Angler's Rest, and the air was fragrant with the
sweet scent of jasmine and tobacco plant. Stars were
peeping out. Blackbirds sang drowsily in the shrub-
beries. Bats wheeled through the shadows, and a
gentle breeze played fitfully among the hollyhocks.
It was, in short, as a customer who had looked in for a
gin and tonic rather happily put it, a nice evening.

Nevertheless, to Mr. Mulliner and the group assembled in the bar parlour of the inn there was a sense of
something missing. It was due to the fact that
Miss Postlethwaite, the efficient barmaid, was absent.
Some forty minutes had elapsed before she arrived
and took over from the pot-boy. When she did so,
the quiet splendour of her costume and the devout
manner in which she pulled the beer-handle told their
own story.

"You've been to church," said a penetrating Sherry
and Angostura.

Miss Postlethwaite said Yes, she had, and it had
been lovely.

"Beautiful in every sense of the word," said Miss
Postlethwaite, filling an order for a pint of bitter. "I

do adore evening service in the summer. It sort of does something to you, what I mean. All that stilly hush and what not."

"The vicar preached the sermon, I suppose?" said Mr. Mulliner.

"Yes," said Miss Postlethwaite, adding that it had been extremely moving.

Mr. Mulliner took a thoughtful sip of his hot Scotch and lemon.

"The old old story," he said, a touch of sadness in his voice. "I do not know if you gentlemen are aware of it, but in the rural districts of England vicars always preach the evening sermon during the summer months, and this causes a great deal of discontent to seethe among curates. It exasperates the young fellows, and one can understand their feelings. As Miss Postlethwaite rightly says, there is something about the atmosphere of evensong in a village church that induces a receptive frame of mind in a congregation, and a preacher, preaching under such conditions, can scarcely fail to grip and stir. The curates, withheld from so preaching, naturally feel that they are being ground beneath the heel of an iron monopoly and chiselled out of their big chance."

A Whisky and Splash said he had never thought of that.

"In that respect," said Mr. Mulliner, "you differ from my cousin Rupert's younger son, Anselm. He thought of it a great deal. He was the curate of the parish of Rising Mattock in Hampshire, and when he was not dreaming fondly of Myrtle Jellaby, niece

of Sir Leopold Jellaby, O.B.E., the local squire, you
would generally find him chafing at his vicar's high-
handed selfishness in always hogging the evening
sermon from late in April till well on in September.
He told me once that it made him feel like a caged
skylark."

"Why did he dream fondly of Myrtle Jellaby?"
asked a Stout and Mild, who was not very quick at
the uptake.

"Because he loved her. And she loved him. She
had, indeed, consented to become his wife."

"They were engaged?" said the Stout and Mild,
beginning to get it.

"Secretly. Anselm did not dare to inform her
uncle of the position of affairs, because all he had to
marry on was his meagre stipend. He feared the
wrath of that millionaire philatelist."

"Millionaire what?" asked a Small Bass.

"Sir Leopold," explained Mr. Mulliner, "collected
stamps."

The Small Bass said that he had always thought
that a philatelist was a man who was kind to animals.

"No," said Mr. Mulliner, "a stamp collector.
Though many philatelists are, I believe, also kind to
animals. Sir Leopold Jellaby had been devoted to
this hobby for many years, ever since he had retired
from business as a promoter of companies in the City
of London. His collection was famous."

"And Anselm didn't like to tell him about Myrtle,"
said the Stout and Mild.

"No. As I say, he lacked the courage. He pursued

instead the cautious policy of lying low and hoping for
the best. And one bright summer day the happy
ending seemed to have arrived. Myrtle, calling at
the vicarage at breakfast-time, found Anselm dancing
round the table, in one hand a half-consumed piece
of toast, in the other a letter, and learned from him that
under the will of his late godfather, the recently
deceased Mr. J. G. Beenstock, he had benefited by an
unexpected legacy—to wit, the stout stamp album
which now lay beside the marmalade dish.

The information caused the girl's face to light up
(continued Mr. Mulliner). A philatelist's niece, she
knew how valuable these things could be.

"What's it worth?" she asked eagerly.

"It is insured, I understand, for no less a sum than
five thousand pounds."

"Golly!"

"Golly, indeed," assented Anselm.

"Nice sugar!" said Myrtle.

"Exceedingly nice," agreed Anselm.

"You must take care of it. Don't leave it lying
about. We don't want somebody pinching it."

A look of pain passed over Anselm's spiritual face.

"You are not suggesting that the vicar would stoop
to such an act?"

"I was thinking more," said Myrtle, "of Joe
Beamish."

She was alluding to a member of her loved one's
little flock who had at one time been a fairly prosperous burglar. Seeing the light after about sixteen

prison sentences, he had given up his life-work, and now raised vegetables and sang in the choir.

"Old Joe is supposed to have reformed and got away from it all, but, if you ask me, there's a lot of life in the old dog yet. If he gets to hear that there's a five-thousand-pound stamp collection lying around. . . ."

"I think you wrong our worthy Joe, darling. However, I will take precautions. I shall place the album in a drawer in the desk in the vicar's study. It is provided with a stout lock. But before doing so, I thought I might take it round and show it to your uncle. It is possible that he may feel disposed to make an offer for the collection."

"That's a thought," agreed Myrtle. "Soak him good."

"I will assuredly omit no effort to that end," said Anselm.

And, kissing Myrtle fondly, he went about his parochial duties.

It was towards evening that he called upon Sir Leopold, and the kindly old squire, learning the nature of his errand and realizing that he had not come to make a touch on behalf of the Church Organ Fund, lost the rather strained look which he had worn when his name was announced and greeted him warmly.

"Stamps?" he said. "Yes, I am always ready to add to my collection, provided that what I am offered is of value and the price reasonable. Had you any figure in mind for these of yours, my dear Mulliner?"

Anselm said that he had been thinking of something in the neighbourhood of five thousand pounds, and Sir Leopold shook from stem to stern like a cat that has received half a brick in the short ribs. All his life the suggestion that he should part with large sums of money had shocked him.

"Oh?" he said. Then, seeming to master himself with a strong effort. "Well, let me look at them."

Ten minutes later, he had closed the volume and was eyeing Anselm compassionately.

"I am afraid you must be prepared for bad news, my boy," he said.

A sickening feeling of apprehension gripped Anselm.

"You don't mean they are not valuable?"

Sir Leopold put the tips of his fingers together and leaned back in his chair in the rather pontifical manner which he had been accustomed to assume in the old days when addressing meetings of shareholders.

"The term 'valuable,' my dear fellow, is a relative one. To some people five pounds would be a large sum."

"Five pounds!"

"That is what I am prepared to offer. Or, seeing that you are a personal friend, shall we say ten?"

"But they are insured for five thousand."

Sir Leopold shook his head with a half-smile.

"My dear Mulliner, if you knew as much as I do about the vanity of stamp collectors, you would not set great store by that. Well, as I say, I don't mind giving you ten pounds for the lot. Think it over and let me know."

On leaden feet Anselm left the room. His hopes

were shattered. He felt like a man who, chasing rainbows, has had one of them suddenly turn and bite him in the leg.

"Well?" said Myrtle, who had been awaiting the result of the conference in the passage.

Anselm broke the sad news. The girl was astounded.

"But you told me the thing was insured for——"

Anselm sighed.

"Your uncle appeared to attribute little or no importance to that. It seems that stamp collectors are in the habit of insuring their collections for fantastic sums, out of a spirit of vanity. I intend," said Anselm, broodingly, "to preach a very strong sermon shortly on the subject of Vanity."

There was a silence.

"Ah, well," said Anselm, "these things are no doubt sent to try us. It is by accepting such blows in a meek and chastened spirit . . ."

"Meek and chastened spirit my left eyeball," cried Myrtle, who, like so many girls to-day, was apt to be unguarded in her speech. "We've got to do something about this."

"But what? I am not denying," said Anselm, "that the shock has been a severe one, and I regret to confess that there was a moment when I was sorely tempted to utter one or two of the observations which I once heard the coach of my college boat at Oxford make to Number Five when he persisted in obtruding his abdomen as he swung his oar. It would have been wrong, but it would unquestionably have relieved my . . ."

"I know!" cried Myrtle. "Joe Beamish!"

Anselm stared at her.

"Joe Beamish? I do not understand you, dear."

"Use your bean, boy, use your bean. You remember what I told you. All we've got to do is let old Joe know where those stamps are, and he will take over from there. And there we shall be with our nice little claim for five thousand of the best on the insurance company."

"Myrtle!"

"It would be money for jam," the enthusiastic girl continued. "Just so much velvet. Go and see Joe at once."

"Myrtle! I beg you, desist. You shock me inexpressibly."

She gazed at him incredulously. "You mean you won't do it?"

"I could not even contemplate such a course."

"You won't unleash old Joe and set him acting for the best?"

"Certainly not. Most decidedly not. A thousand times, no."

"But what's wrong with the idea?"

"The whole project is ethically unsound."

There was a pause. For a moment it seemed as if the girl was about to express her chagrin in an angry outburst. A frown darkened her brow, and she kicked petulantly at a passing beetle. Then she appeared to get the better of her emotion. Her face cleared, and she smiled at him tenderly, like a mother at her fractious child.

"Oh, all right. Just as you say. Where are you off to now?"

"I have a Mothers' Meeting at six."

"And I," said Myrtle, "have got to take a few pints of soup to the deserving poor. I'd better set about it. Amazing the way these bimbos absorb soup. Like sponges."

They walked together as far as the Village Hall. Anselm went in to meet the Mothers. Myrtle, as soon as he was out of sight, turned and made her way to Joe Beamish's cosy cottage. The crooning of a hymn from within showing that its owner was at home, she walked through its honeysuckle-covered porch.

"Well, Joe, old top," she said, "how's everything?"

Joe Beamish was knitting a sock in the tiny living-room which smelled in equal proportions of mice, ex-burglars and shag tobacco, and Myrtle, as her gaze fell upon his rugged features, felt her heart leap within her like that of the poet Wordsworth when beholding a rainbow in the sky. His altered circumstances had not changed the erstwhile porch-climber's outward appearance. It remained that of one of those men for whom the police are always spreading drag-nets; and Myrtle, eyeing him, had the feeling that in supposing that in this pre-eminent plugugly there still lurked something of the Old Adam, she had called her shots correctly.

For some minutes after her entry, the conversation was confined to neutral topics—the weather, the sock and the mice behind the wainscoting. It was only when it turned to the decorations of the church for the forthcoming Harvest Festival—to which, she learned, her host would be in a position to contribute two cabbages and a pumpkin—that Myrtle saw her opportunity of approaching a more intimate subject.

"Mr. Mulliner will be pleased about that," she said. "He's nuts on the Harvest Festival."

"R," said Joe Beamish. "He's a good man, Mr. Mulliner."

"He's a lucky man," said Myrtle. "Have you heard what's just happened to him? Some sort of deceased Beenstock has gone and left him five thousand quid."

"Coo! Is that right?"

"Well, it comes to the same thing. An album of stamps that's worth five thousand. You know how valuable stamps are. Why, my uncle's collection is worth ten times that. That's why we've got all those burglar alarms up at the Hall."

A rather twisted expression came into Joe Beamish's face.

"I've heard there's a lot of burglar alarms up at the Hall," he said.

"But there aren't any at the vicarage, and, between you and me, Joe, it's worrying me rather. Because, you see, that's where Mr. Mulliner is keeping his stamps."

"R," said Joe Beamish, speaking now with a thoughtful intonation.

"I told him he ought to keep them at his bank."

Joe Beamish started.

"Wot ever did you go and say a silly thing like that for?" he asked.

"It wasn't at all silly," said Myrtle warmly. "It was just ordinary common sense. I don't consider those stamps are safe, left lying in a drawer in the desk in the vicar's study, that little room on the ground floor to the right of the front door with its flimsy French windows that could so easily be forced with a chisel or something. They are locked up, of course, but what good are locks? I've seen these, and anybody could open them with a hairpin. I tell you, Joe, I'm worried."

Joe Beamish bent over his sock, knitting and purling for a while in silence. When he spoke again, it was to talk of pumpkins and cabbages, and after that, for he was a man of limited ideas, of cabbages and pumpkins.

Anselm Mulliner, meanwhile, was passing through a day of no little spiritual anguish. At the moment when it had been made, Myrtle's proposal had shaken him to his foundations. He had not felt so utterly unmanned since the evening when he had been giving young Willie Purvis a boxing lesson at the Lad's Club, and Willie, by a happy accident, had got home squarely on the button.

This revelation of the character of the girl to whom he had given a curate's unspotted heart had stunned him. Myrtle, it seemed to him, appeared to have no notion whatsoever of the distinction between right and wrong. And while this would not have mattered, of course, had be been a gun-man and she his prospective moll, it made a great deal of difference to one who hoped later on to become a vicar and, in such event, would want his wife to look after the parish funds. He wondered what the prophet Isaiah would have had to say about it, had he been informed of her views on strategy and tactics.

All through the afternoon and evening he continued to brood on the thing. At supper that night he was distrait and preoccupied. Busy with his own reflections, he scarcely listened to the conversation of the Rev. Sidney Gooch, his vicar. And this was perhaps fortunate, for it was a Saturday and the vicar, as was his custom at Saturday suppers, harped a good deal on the subject of the sermon which he was proposing to deliver at evensong on the morrow. He said, not once but many times, that he confidently expected, if the fine weather held up, to knock his little flock cockeyed. The Rev. Sidney was a fine, upstanding specimen of the muscular Christian, but somewhat deficient in tact.

Towards nightfall, however, Anselm found a kindlier, mellower note creeping into his meditations. Possibly it was the excellent round of beef of which he had partaken, and the wholesome ale with which he had washed it down, that caused this softer mood. As he smoked his after-supper cigarette, he found himself beginning to relax in his austere attitude towards Myrtle's feminine weakness. He reminded himself that it must be placed to her credit that she had not been obdurate. On the contrary, the moment he had made plain his disapproval of her financial methods, conscience had awakened, her better self had prevailed and she had abandoned her dubious schemes. That was much.

Happy once more, he went to bed and, after dipping into a good book for half an hour, switched off the light and fell into a restful sleep.

But it seemed to him that he had scarcely done so when he was wakened by loud noises. He sat up, listening. Something in the nature of a free-for-all appeared to be in progress in the lower part of the house. His knowledge of the vicarage's topography suggested to him that the noises were proceeding from the study and, hastily donning a dressing-gown, he made his way thither.

The room was in darkness, but he found the switch and, turning on the light, perceived that the odd, groaning sound which had greeted him as he approached the door proceeded from the Rev. Sidney Gooch. The vicar was sitting on the floor, a hand pressed to his left eye.

"A burglar!" he said, rising. "A beastly bounder of a burglar."

"He has injured you, I fear," said Anselm, commiseratingly.

"Of course he has injured me," said the Rev. Sidney, with some testiness. "Can a man take fire in his bosom and his clothes not be burned? Proverbs, six, twenty-seven. I heard a sound and came down and seized the fellow, and he struck me so violently that I was compelled to loosen my grip, and he made his escape through the window. Be so kind, Mulliner, as to look about and see if he has taken anything.

There were some manuscript sermons which I should not care to lose."

Anselm was standing beside the desk. He had to pause for a moment in order to control his voice.

"The only object that appears to have been removed," he said, "is an album of stamps belonging to myself."

"The sermons are there?"

"Still there."

"Bitter," said the vicar. "Bitter."

"I beg your pardon?" said Anselm.

He turned. His superior of the cloth was standing before the mirror, regarding himself in it with a rueful stare.

"Bitter!" he repeated. "I was thinking," he explained, "of the one I had planned to deliver at evensong to-morrow. A pippin, Mulliner, in the deepest and truest sense a pippin. I am not exaggerating when I say that I would have had them tearing up the pews. And now that dream is ended. I cannot possibly appear in the pulpit with a shiner like this. It would put wrong ideas into the heads of the congregation—always, in these rural communities, so prone to place the worst construction on such disfigurements. To-morrow, Mulliner, I shall be confined to my bed with a slight chill, and you will conduct both matins and evensong. Bitter!" said the Rev. Sidney Gooch. "Bitter!"

Anselm did not speak. His heart was too full for words.

In Anselm's deportment and behaviour on the

following morning there was nothing to indicate that his soul was a maelstrom of seething emotions. Most curates who find themselves unexpectedly allowed to preach on Sunday evening in the summer time are like dogs let off the chain. They leap. They bound. They sing snatches of the more rollicking psalms. They rush about saying "Good morning, good morning," to everybody and patting children on the head. Not so Anselm. He knew that only by conserving his nervous energies would he be able to give of his best when the great moment came.

To those of the congregation who were still awake in the later stages of the service his sermon at Matins seemed dull and colourless. And so it was. He had no intention of frittering away eloquence on a morning sermon. He deliberately held himself back, concentrating every fibre of his being on the address which he was to deliver in the evening.

He had had it by him for months. Every curate throughout the English countryside keeps tucked away among his effects a special sermon designed to prevent him being caught short, if suddenly called upon to preach at evensong. And all through the afternoon he remained closeted in his room, working upon it. He pruned. He polished. He searched the Thesaurus for the telling adjective. By the time the church bells began to ring out over the fields and spinneys of Rising Mattock in the quiet gloaming, his masterpiece was perfected to the last comma.

Feeling more like a volcano than a curate, Anselm

K

Mulliner pinned together the sheets of manuscript and set forth.

The conditions could not have been happier. By the end of the pre-sermon hymn the twilight was far advanced, and through the door of the little church there poured the scent of trees and flowers. All was still, save for the distant tinkling of sheep bells and the drowsy calling of rooks among the elms. With quiet confidence Anselm mounted the pulpit steps. He had been sucking throat pastilles all day and saying "Mi-mi" to himself in an undertone throughout the service, and he knew that he would be in good voice.

For an instant he paused and gazed about him. He was rejoiced to see that he was playing to absolute capacity. Every pew was full. There, in the squire's high-backed stall, was Sir Leopold Jellaby, O.B.E., with Myrtle at his side. There, among the choir, looking indescribably foul in a surplice, sat Joe Beamish. There, in their respective places, were the butcher, the baker, the candlestick-maker and all the others who made up the personnel of the congregation. With a little sigh of rapture, Anselm cleared his throat and gave out the simple text of Brotherly Love.

I have been privileged (said Mr. Mulliner) to read the script of this sermon of Anselm's, and it must, I can see, have been extremely powerful. Even in manuscript form, without the added attraction of the young man's beautifully modulated tenor voice, one can clearly sense its magic.

Beginning with a thoughtful excursus on Brotherly

Love among the Hivites and Hittites, it came down through the Early Britons, the Middle Ages and the spacious days of Queen Elizabeth to these modern times of ours, and it was here that Anselm Mulliner really let himself go. It was at this point, if one may employ the phrase, that he—in the best and most reverent spirit of the words—reached for the accelerator and stepped on it.

Earnestly, in accents throbbing with emotion, he spoke of our duty to one another; of the task that lies clear before all of us to make this a better and a sweeter world for our fellows; of the joy that waits those who give no thought to self but strain every nerve to do the square thing by one and all. And with each golden phrase he held his audience in an ever-tightening grip. Tradesmen who had been nodding somnolently woke up and sat with parted lips. Women dabbed at their eyes with handkerchiefs. Choir-boys who had been sucking acid drops swallowed them remorsefully and stopped shuffling their feet.

Even at a morning service, such a sermon would have been a smash hit. Delivered in the gloaming, with all its adventitious aids to success, it was a riot.

It was not immediately after the conclusion of the proceedings that Anselm was able to tear himself away from the crowd of admirers that surged round him in the vestry. There were churchwardens who wanted to shake his hand, other churchwardens who insisted on smacking him on the back. One even asked for his autograph. But eventually he laughingly shook himself free and made his way back to the

vicarage. And scarcely had he passed through the
garden gate when something shot out at him from
the scented darkness, and he found Myrtle Jellaby in
his arms.

"Anselm!" she cried. "My wonder-man! However did you do it? I never heard such a sermon in
my life!"

"It got across, I think?" said Anselm modestly.

"It was terrific. Golly! When you admonish a
congregation, it stays admonished. How you think
of all these things beats me."

"Oh, they come to one."

"And another thing I can't understand is how you
came to be preaching at all in the evening. I thought
you told me the vicar always did."

"The vicar," began Anselm, "has met with a
slight . . ."

And then it suddenly occurred to him that in the
excitement of being allowed to preach at evensong he
had quite forgotten to inform Myrtle of that other
important happening, the theft of the stamp album.

"A rather extraordinary thing occurred last night,
darling," he said. "The vicarage was burgled."

Myrtle was amazed.

"Not really?"

"Yes. A marauder broke in through the study
window."

"Well, fancy that! Did he take anything?"

"He took my collection of stamps."

Myrtle uttered a cry of ecstasy.

"Then we collect!"

Anselm did not speak for a moment.

"I wonder."

"What do you mean, you wonder? Of course we collect. Shoot the claim in to the insurance people without a moment's delay."

"But have you reflected, dearest? Am I justified in doing as you suggest?"

"Of course. Why ever not?"

"It seems to me a moot point. The collection, we know, is worthless. Can I justly demand of this firm—The London and Midland Counties Aid and Benefit Association is its name—that they pay me five thousand pounds for an album of stamps that is without value?"

"Of course you can. Old Beenstock paid the premiums, didn't he?"

"That is true. Yes, I had forgotten that."

"It doesn't matter whether a thing's valuable or not. The point is what you insure it for. And it isn't as if it's going to hurt these Mutual Aid and Benefit birds to brass up. It's sinful the amount of money those insurance companies have. Must be jolly bad for them, if you ask me."

Anselm had not thought of that. Examining the point now, it seemed to him that Myrtle, with her woman's intuition, had rather gone to the root of the matter and touched the spot.

Was there not, he asked himself, a great deal to be said for this theory of hers that insurance companies had much too much money and would be better, finer, more spiritual insurance companies if somebody came

along occasionally and took a bit of the stuff off them?
Unquestionably there was.   His doubts were removed.
He saw now that it was not only a pleasure, but a
duty, to nick the London and Midland Counties Mutual
Aid and Benefit Association for five thousand.   It
might prove the turning-point in the lives of its Board
of Directors.

"Very well," he said.   "I will send in the claim."

"At-a-boy!   And the instant we touch, we'll get
married."

"Myrtle!"

"Anselm!"

"Guv'nor," said the voice of Joe Beamish at their
side, "could I 'ave a word with you?"

They drew apart with a start, and stared dumbly
at the man.

"Guv'nor," said Joe Beamish, and it was plain
from the thickness of his utterance that he was in the
grip of some strong emotion, "I want to thank you,
guv'nor, for that there sermon of yours.   That there
wonderful sermon."

Anselm smiled.   He had recovered from the shock
of hearing this sudden voice in the night.   It was a
nuisance, of course, to be interrupted like this at
such a moment, but one must, he felt, be courteous
to the fans.   No doubt he would have to expect a lot
of this sort of thing from now on.

"I am rejoiced that my poor effort should have
elicited so striking an ecomium."

"Wot say?"

"He says he's glad you liked it," said Myrtle, a

little irritably, for she was not feeling her most amiable. A young girl who is nestling in the arms of the man she loves resents having cracksmen popping up through traps at her elbow.

"R," said Joe Beamish, enlightened. "Yes, guv'nor, that was a sermon, that was. That was what I call a blinking sermon."

"Thank you, Joe, thank you. It is nice to feel that you were pleased."

"You're right, I was pleased, guv'nor. I've 'eard sermons in Pentonville, and I've 'eard sermons in Wormwood Scrubs, and I've 'eard sermons in Dartmoor, and very good sermons they were, but of all the sermons I've 'eard I never 'eard a sermon that could touch this 'ere sermon for class and pep and . . ."

"Joe," said Myrtle.

"Yes, lady?"

"Scram!"

"Pardon, lady?"

"Get out. Pop off. Buzz along. Can't you see you're not wanted? We're busy."

"My dear," said Anselm, with gentle reproach, "is not your manner a little peremptory? I would not have the honest fellow feel . . ."

"R," interrupted Joe Beamish, and there was a suggestion of unshed tears in his voice, "but I'm not an honest feller, guv'nor. There, if you don't mind me saying so, no offence meant and none, I 'ope, taken, is where you make your bloomin' error. I'm a pore sinner and backslider and evildoer and . . ."

"Joe," said Myrtle, with a certain menacing calm,

"if you get a thick ear, always remember that you asked for it. The same applies to a lump the size of an egg on top of your ugly head through coming into violent contact with the knob of my parasol. Will you or will you not," she said, taking a firmer grip of the handle of the weapon to which she had alluded, "push off?"

"Lady," said Joe Beamish, not without a rough dignity, "as soon as I've done what I come to do, I will withdraw. But first I got to do what I come to do. And what I come to do is 'and back in a meek and contrite spirit this 'ere album of stamps what I snitched last night, never thinking that I was to 'ear that there wonderful sermon and see the light. But 'avin' 'eard that there wonderful sermon and seen the light, I now 'ave great pleasure in doing what I come to do, namely," said Joe Beamish, thrusting the late J. G. Beenstock's stamp collection into Anselm's hand, "this 'ere. Lady . . . Guv'nor . . . With these few words, 'opin' that you are in the pink as it leaves me at present, I will now withdraw."

"Stop!" cried Anselm.

"R?"

Anselm's face was strangely contorted. He spoke with difficulty.

"Joe. . . ."

"Yes, guv'nor?"

"Joe . . . I would like . . . I would prefer . . . In a very real sense I do so feel . . . In short, I would like you to keep this stamp album, Joe."

The burglar shook his head.

"No, guv'nor. It can't be done. When I think of that there wonderful sermon and all those beautiful things you said in that there wonderful sermon about the 'Ivites and the 'Ittites and doing the right thing by the neighbours and 'elping so far as in you lies to spread sweetness and light throughout the world, I can't keep no albums which 'ave come into my possession through gettin' in at other folks' French winders on account of not 'avin' seen the light. It don't belong to me, not that album don't, and I now take much pleasure in 'andin' it back with these few words. Goo' night, guv'nor. Goo' night, lady. Goo' night, all. I will now withdraw."

His footsteps died away, and there was silence in the quiet garden. Both Anselm and Myrtle were busy with their thoughts. Once more through Anselm's mind there was racing that pithy address which the coach of his college boat had delivered when trying to do justice to the spectacle of Number Five's obtrusive stomach: while Myrtle, on her side, was endeavouring not to give utterance to a rough translation of something she had once heard a French taxi-driver say to a gendarme during her finishing-school days in Paris.

Anselm was the first to speak.

"This, dearest," he said, "calls for discussion. One does so feel that little or nothing can be accomplished without earnest thought and a frank round-table conference. Let us go indoors and thresh the whole matter out in as calm a spirit as we can achieve."

He led the way to the study and seated himself

moodily, his chin in his hands, his brow furrowed. A deep sigh escaped him.

"I understand now," he said, "why it is that curates are not permitted to preach on Sunday evenings during the summer months. It is not safe. It is like exploding a bomb in a public place. It upsets existing conditions too violently. When I reflect that, had our good vicar but been able to take evensong to-night, this distressing thing would not have occurred, I find myself saying in the words of the prophet Hosea to the children of Adullam . . ."

"Putting the prophet Hosea to one side for the moment and temporarily pigeon-holing the children of Adullam," interrupted Myrtle, "what are we going to do about this?"

Anselm sighed again.

"Alas, dearest, there you have me. I assume that it is no longer feasible to submit a claim to the London and Midland Counties Mutual Aid and Benefit Association."

"So we lose five thousand of the best and brightest?"

Anselm winced. The lines deepened on his careworn face.

"It is not an agreeable thing to contemplate, I agree. One had been looking on the sum as one's little nest-egg. One did so want to see it safely in the bank, to be invested later in sound, income-bearing securities. I confess to feeling a little vexed with Joe Beamish."

"I hope he chokes."

"I would not go so far as that, darling," said Anselm,

with loving rebuke. "But I must admit that if I heard that he had tripped over a loose shoelace and sprained his ankle, it would—in the deepest and truest sense—be all right with me. I deplore the man's tactless impulsiveness. 'Officious' is the word that springs to the lips."

Myrtle was musing.

"Listen," she said. "Why not play a little joke on these London and Midland bozos? Why tell them you've got the stamps back? Why not just sit tight and send in the claim and pouch their cheque? That would be a lot of fun."

Again, for the second time in two days, Anselm found himself looking a little askance at his loved one. Then he reminded himself that she was scarcely to be blamed for her somewhat unconventional outlook. The niece of a prominent financier, she was perhaps entitled to be somewhat eccentric in her views. No doubt, her earliest childhood memories were of coming down to dessert and hearing her elders discuss over the nuts and wine some burgeoning scheme for trimming the investors.

He shook his head.

"I could hardly countenance such a policy, I fear. To me there seems something—I do not wish to hurt your feelings, dearest—something almost dishonest about what you suggest. Besides," he added, meditatively, "when Joe Beamish handed back that album, he did it in the presence of witnesses."

"Witnesses?"

"Yes, dearest. As we came into the house, I

observed a shadowy figure. Whose it was, I cannot say, but of this I feel convinced—that this person, whoever he may have been, heard all."

"You're sure?"

"Quite sure. He was standing beneath the cedar-tree, within easy earshot. And, as you know, our worthy Beamish's voice is of a robust and carrying timbre."

He broke off. Unable to restrain her pent-up feelings any longer, Myrtle Jellaby had uttered the words which the taxi-driver had said to the gendarme, and there was that about them which might well have rendered a tougher curate than Anselm temporarily incapable of speech. A throbbing silence followed the ejaculation. And during this silence there came to their ears from the garden without a curious sound.

"Hark," said Myrtle.

They listened. What they heard was unmistakably a human being sobbing.

"Some fellow creature in trouble," said Anselm.

"Thank goodness," said Myrtle.

"Should we go and ascertain the sufferer's identity?"

"Let's," said Myrtle. "I have an idea it may be Joe Beamish. In which case, what I am going to do to him with my parasol will be nobody's business."

But the mourner was not Joe Beamish, who had long since gone off to the Goose and Grasshopper. To Anselm, who was shortsighted, the figure leaning against the cedar-tree, shaking with uncontrollable sobs, was indistinct and unrecognizable, but Myrtle, keener-eyed, uttered a cry of surprise.

"Uncle!"

"Uncle?" said Anselm, astonished.

"It is Uncle Leopold."

"Yes," said the O.B.E., choking down a groan and moving away from the tree, "it is I. Is that Mulliner standing beside you, Myrtle?"

"Yes."

"Mulliner," said Sir Leopold Jellaby, "you find me in tears. And why am I in tears? Because, my dear Mulliner, I am still overwhelmed by that wonderful sermon of yours on Brotherly Love and our duty to our neighbours."

Anselm began to wonder if ever a curate had had notices like these.

"Oh, thanks," he said, shuffling a foot. "Awfully glad you liked it."

"'Liked it,' Mulliner, is a weak term. That sermon has revolutionized my entire outlook. It has made me a different man. I wonder, Mulliner, if you can find me pen and ink inside the house?"

"Pen and ink?"

"Precisely. I wish to write you a cheque for ten thousand pounds for that stamp collection of yours."

"Ten thousand!"

"Come inside," said Myrtle. "Come right in."

"You see," said Sir Leopold, as they led him to the study and plied him with many an eager query as to whether he preferred a thick nib or a thin, "when you showed me those stamps yesterday, I recognized their value immediately—they would fetch five thousand pounds anywhere—so I naturally told you they were worthless. It was one of those ordinary, routine business precautions which a man is bound to take. One of the first things I remember my dear father saying to me, when he sent me out to battle with the world, was 'Never give a sucker an even break,' and until now I have always striven not to do so. But your sermon to-night has made me see that there is something higher and nobler than a code of business ethics. Shall I cross the cheque?"

"If you please."

"No," said Myrtle. "Make it open."

"Just as you say, my dear. You appear," said the kind old squire, smiling archly through his tears, "to be showing considerable interest in the matter. Am I to infer——?"

"I love Anselm. We are engaged."

"Mulliner! Is this so?"

"Er—yes," said Anselm. "I was meaning to tell you about that."

Sir Leopold patted him on the shoulder.

"I could wish her no better husband. There. There is your cheque, Mulliner. The collection, as I say, is worth five thousand pounds, but after that sermon, I give ten freely—freely!"

Anselm, like one in a dream, took the oblong slip of paper and put it in his pocket. Silently, he handed the album to Sir Leopold.

"Thank you," said the latter. "And now, my dear fellow, I think I shall have to ask you for the loan of a clean pocket handkerchief. My own, as you see, is completely saturated."

It was while Anselm was in his room, rummaging in the chest of drawers, that a light footstep caused him to turn. Myrtle was standing in the doorway, a finger on her lip.

"Anselm," she whispered, "have you a fountain-pen?"

"Certainly, dearest. There should be one in this drawer. Yes, here it is. You wish to write something?"

"I wish you to write something. Endorse that cheque here and now, and give it to me, and I will motor to London to-night in my two-seater, so as to be at the bank the moment it opens and deposit it. You see, I know Uncle Leopold. He might take it into his head, after he had slept on it and that sermon had worn off a bit, to 'phone and stop payment. You know how he feels about business precautions. This way we shall avoid all rannygazoo."

Anselm kissed her fondly.

"You think of everything, dearest," he said. "How right you are. One does so wish, does one not, to avoid rannygazoo."

ROMANCE AT DROITGATE SPA

ROMANCE AT DROITGATE SPA

WHEN young Freddie Fitch-Fitch went down to Droitgate Spa, that celebrated cure resort in the west of England, to ask his uncle and trustee, Major-General Sir Aylmer Bastable, to release his capital in order that he might marry Annabel Purvis, he was fully alive to the fact that the interview might prove a disagreeable one. However, his great love bore him on, and he made the journey and was shown into the room where the old man sat nursing a gouty foot.

"Hullo-ullo-ullo, uncle," he cried, for it was always his policy on these occasions to be buoyant till thrown out. "Good morning, good morning, good morning."

"Gaw!" said Sir Aylmer, with a sort of long, shuddering sigh. "It's you, is it?"

And he muttered something which Freddie did not quite catch, though he was able to detect the words "last straw."

Freddie's heart sank a little. He could see that his flesh and blood was in difficult mood, and he guessed what must have happened. No doubt Sir Aylmer had been to the Pump Room earlier in the day to take the waters, and while there had met and been high-hatted by some swell whom the doctors had twice given up for dead. These snobs, he knew, were always snubbing the unfortunate old man.

On coming to settle in Droitgate Spa, Sir Aylmer Bastable had had a humiliating shock. The head of a fine old family and the possessor of a distinguished military record, he had expected on his arrival to be received with open arms by the best people and welcomed immediately into the inner set. But when it was discovered that all he had wrong with him was a touch of gout in the right foot, he found himself cold-shouldered by the men who mattered and thrust back on the society of the asthma patients and the fellows with slight liver trouble.

For though few people are aware of it—so true is it that half the world does not know how the other half lives—there is no section of the community in which class-consciousness is so rampant as among invalids. The ancient Spartans, one gathers, were far from cordial towards their Helots, and the French aristocrat of pre-Revolution days tended to be a little stand-offish with his tenantry, but their attitude was almost back-slapping compared with that of— let us say—the man who has been out in Switzerland taking insulin for his diabetes towards one who is simply undergoing treatment from the village doctor for an ingrowing toe-nail. And this is particularly so, of course, in those places where invalids collect in gangs—Baden-Baden, for example, or Hot Springs, Virginia, or, as in Sir Aylmer's case, Droitgate Spa.

In such resorts the atmosphere is almost unbelievably cliquy. The old aristocracy, the top-notchers with maladies that get written up in the medical journals, keep themselves to themselves pretty rigidly, and have a very short way with the smaller fry.

It was this that had soured Sir Aylmer Bastable's once sunny disposition and caused him now to glare at Freddie with an unfriendly eye.

"Well," he said, "what do you want?"

"Oh, I just looked in," said Freddie. "How's everything?"

"Rotten," replied Sir Aylmer. "I've just lost my nurse."

"Dead?"

"Worse. Married. The cloth-headed girl has gone off and got spliced to one of the *canaille*—a chap who's never even had so much as athlete's foot. She must be crazy."

"Still, one sees her point of view."

"No, one doesn't."

"I mean," said Freddie, who felt strongly on this subject, "it's love that makes the world go round."

"It isn't anything of the kind," said Sir Aylmer. Like so many fine old soldiers, he was inclined to be a little literal-minded. "I never heard such dashed silly nonsense in my life. What makes the world go round is . . . Well, I've forgotten at the moment, but it certainly isn't love. How the dooce could it?"

"Oh, right-ho. I see what you mean," said Freddie. "But put it another way. Love conquers all. Love's all right. Take it from me."

The old man looked at him sharply.

"Are you in love?"

"Madly."

"Of all the young cuckoos! And I suppose you've come to ask for money to get married on?"

"Not at all. I just dropped round to see how you were. Still, as the subject has happened to crop up——"

Sir Aylmer brooded for a moment, snorting in an undertone.

"Who's the girl?" he demanded.

Freddie coughed, and fumbled with his collar. The crux of the situation, he realized, had now been reached. He had feared from the first that this was where the good old snag might conceivably sidle into the picture. For his Annabel was of humble station, and he knew how rigid were his relative's views on the importance of birth. No bigger snob ever swallowed a salicylate pill.

"Well, as a matter of fact," he said, "she's a conjurer's stooge."

"A *what*?"

"A conjurer's assistant, don't you know. I saw her first at a charity matinée. She was abetting a bloke called The Great Boloni."

"In what sense, abetting?"

"Well, she stood there up-stage, don't you know, and every now and then she would skip down-stage, hand this chap a bowl of goldfish or something, beam at the audience, do a sort of dance step and skip back again. You know the kind of thing."

A dark frown had come into Sir Aylmer's face.

"I do," he said grimly. "My only nephew has

been ensnared by a bally, beaming goldfish-hander!
Ha!"

"I wouldn't call it ensnared exactly," said Freddie
deferentially.

"I would," said Sir Aylmer. "Get out of here."

"Right," said Freddie, and caught the 2.35 express
back to London. And it was during the journey that
an idea flashed upon him.

The last of the Fitch-Fitches was not a great student
of literature, but he occasionally dipped into a magazine: and everybody who has ever dipped into a
magazine has read a story about a hard-hearted old
man who won't accept the hero's girl at any price, so
what do they do but plant her on him without telling
him who she is and, by Jove, he falls under her spell
completely, and then they tear off their whiskers and
there they are. There was a story of this nature in the
magazine which Freddie had purchased at the book-
stall at Droitgate Spa Station, and, as he read it, he
remembered what his uncle had told him about his
nurse handing in her portfolio.

By the time the train checked in at Paddington, his
plans were fully formed.

"Listen," he said to Annabel Purvis, who had met
him at the terminus, and Annabel said: "What?"

"Listen," said Freddie, and Annabel again said:
"What?"

"Listen," said Freddie, clasping her arm tenderly
and steering her off in the direction of the refreshment-
room, where it was his intention to have a quick one.

"To a certain extent I am compelled to admit that my
expedition has been a wash-out . . ."

Annabel caught her breath sharply.

"No blessing?"

"No blessing."

"And no money?"

"No money. The old boy ran entirely true to stable
form. He listened to what I had to say, snorted in an
unpleasant manner and threw me out. The old
routine. But what I'm working round to is that the
skies are still bright and the blue bird on the job. I
have a scheme. Could you be a nurse?"

"I used to nurse my Uncle Joe."

"Then you shall nurse my Uncle Aylmer. The
present incumbent, he tells me, has just tuned out, and
he needs a successor. I will 'phone him that I am
dispatching immediately a red-hot nurse whom he
will find just the same as Mother makes, and you
shall go down to Droitgate Spa and ingratiate
yourself."

"But how?"

"Why, cluster round him. Smooth his pillow.
Bring him cooling drinks. Coo to him, and give him
the old oil. Tell him you are of gentle birth, if that's
the expression I want. And when the time is ripe,
when you have entwined yourself about his heart and
he looks upon you as a daughter, shoot me a wire and
I'll come down and fall in love with you and he will
give us his consent, blessing and the stuff. I guarantee
this plan. It works."

So Annabel went to Droitgate Spa, and about three

weeks later a telegram arrived for Freddie, running
as follows:

"*Have ingratiated self. Come at once. Love and
kisses. Annabel.*"

Within an hour of its arrival, Freddie was on his
way to Podagra Lodge, his uncle's residence.

He found Sir Aylmer in his study. Annabel was
sitting by his side, reading aloud to him from a recently
published monograph on certain obscure ailments of
the medulla oblongata. For the old man, though a
mere gout patient, had pathetic aspirations towards
higher things. There was a cooling drink on the table,
and, as Freddie entered, the girl paused in her reading
to smooth her employer's pillow.

"Gaw!" said Sir Aylmer. "You again?"

"Here I am," said Freddie.

"Well, by an extraordinary chance, I'm glad to see
you. Leave us for a moment, Miss Purvis. I wish to
speak to my nephew here, such as he is, on a serious
and private matter. Did you notice that girl?" he
said, as the door closed.

"I did, indeed."

"Pretty."

"An eyeful."

"And as good," said Sir Aylmer, "as she is beautiful.
You should see her smooth pillows. And what a
cooling drink she mixes! Excellent family, too, I
understand. Her father is a colonel. Or, rather, was.
He's dead."

"Ah, well, all flesh is as grass."

"No, it isn't. It's nothing of the kind. The two things are entirely different. I've seen flesh and I've seen grass. No resemblance whatever. However, that is not the point at issue. What I wanted to say was that if you were not a damn fool, that's the sort of girl you would be in love with."

"I am."

"A damn fool?"

"No. In love with that girl."

"What! You have fallen in love with Miss Purvis? Already?"

"I have."

"Well, that's the quickest thing I ever saw. What about your beaming goldfish?"

"Oh, that's all over. A mere passing boyish fancy."

Sir Aylmer took a deep swig at his cooling drink, and regarded him in silence for a moment.

"Well," he said, at length, breathing heavily, "if that's the airy, casual way in which you treat life's most sacred emotions, the sooner you are safely married and settled down, the better. If you're allowed to run around loose much longer, indulging those boyish fancies of yours, I foresee the breach of promise case of the century. However, I'm not saying I'm not relieved. I am relieved. I suppose she wore tights, this goldfish girl?"

"Pink."

"Disgusting. Thank God it's all over. Very good, then. You are free, I understand, to have a pop at Miss Purvis. Do you propose to do so?"

"I do."

"Excellent. You get that sweet, refined, most-suitable-in-all-respects girl to marry you, and I'll hand over that money of yours, every penny of it."

"I will start at once."

"Heaven speed your wooing," said Sir Aylmer.

And ten minutes later Freddie was able to inform his uncle that his whirlwind courtship had been successful, and Sir Aylmer said that when he had asked Heaven to speed his wooing he had had no notion that it would speed it to quite that extent. He congratulated Freddie warmly and said he hoped that he appreciated his good fortune, and Freddie said he certainly did, because his love was like a red, red rose, and Sir Aylmer said "No, she wasn't," and when Freddie added that he was walking on air Sir Aylmer said he couldn't be— the thing was physically impossible.

However, he gave his blessing and promised to release Freddie's capital as soon as the necessary papers were drawn up, and Freddie went back to London to see his lawyer about this.

His mood, as the train sped through the quiet countryside, was one of perfect tranquillity and happiness. It seemed to him that his troubles were now definitely ended. He looked down the vista of the years and saw nothing but joy and sunshine. If somebody had told Frederick Fitch-Fitch at that moment that even now a V-shaped depression was coming along which would shortly blacken the skies and lower the general temperature to freezing-point, he would not have believed him.

Nor when, two days later, as he sat in his club, he was informed that a Mr. Rackstraw was waiting to see him in the small smoking-room, did he have an inkling that here was the V-shaped depression in person. His heart was still light as he went down the passage, wondering idly, for the name was unfamiliar to him, who this Mr. Rackstraw might be. He entered the room, and found there a tall, thin man with pointed black moustaches who was pacing up and down, nervously taking rabbits out of his top-hat as he walked.

"Mr. Rackstraw?"

His visitor spun round, dropping a rabbit. He gazed at Freddie piercingly. He had bright, glittering, sinister eyes.

"That is my name. Mortimer Rackstraw."

Freddie's mind had flown back to the charity matinée at which he had first seen Annabel, and he recognized the fellow now.

"The Great Boloni, surely?"

"I call myself that professionally. So you are Mr. Fitch? So *you* are Mr. Fitch? Ha! Fiend!"

"Eh?"

"I am not mistaken. You are Frederick Fitch?"

"Frederick Fitch-Fitch."

"I beg your pardon. In that case, I should have said 'Fiend! Fiend!'"

He produced a pack of cards and asked Freddie to take one—any one—and memorize it and put it back. Freddie did so absently. He was considerably fogged. He could make nothing of all this.

"How do you mean—Fiend-Fiend?" he asked.

The other sneered unpleasantly.

"Cad!" he said, twirling his moustache.

"Cad?" said Freddie, mystified.

"Yes, sir. Cad. You have stolen the girl I love."

"I don't understand."

"Then you must be a perfect ass. It's quite simple, isn't it? I can't put it any plainer, can I? I say you have stolen . . . Well, look here," said Mortimer Rackstraw. "Suppose this top-hat is me. This rabbit," he went on, producing it from the lining, "is the girl I love. You come along and—presto—the rabbit vanishes.

"It's up your sleeve."

"It is not up my sleeve. And if it were, if I had a thousand sleeves and rabbits up every one of them, that would not alter the fact that you have treacherously robbed me of Annabel Purvis."

Freddie began to see daylight. He was able to appreciate the other's emotion. "So you love Annabel, too?"

"I do."

"I don't wonder. Nice girl, what? I see, I see. You worshipped her in secret, never telling your love."

"I did tell my love. We were engaged."

"Engaged?"

"Certainly. And this morning I get a letter from her saying that it's all off, because she has changed her mind and is going to marry you. She has thrown me over."

"Oh, ah? Well, I'm frightfully sorry—deepest

sympathy, and all that, but I don't see what's to be done about it, what?"

"I do. There still remains—revenge."

"Oh, I say, dash it! You aren't going to be stuffy about it?"

"I am going to be stuffy about it. For the moment you triumph. But do not imagine that this is the end. You have not heard the last of me. Not by any means. You may have stolen the woman I love with your underhand chicanery, but I'll fix you."

"How?"

"Never mind how. You will find out how quite soon enough. A nasty jolt you're going to get, my good fiend, and almost immediately. As sure," said Mortimer Rackstraw, illustrating by drawing one from Freddie's back hair, "as eggs are eggs. I wish you a very good afternoon."

He took up his top-hat, which in his emotion he had allowed to fall to the ground, brushed it on his coat-sleeve, extracted from it a cage of love-birds and strode out.

A moment later, he returned, bowed a few times to right and left and was gone again.

To say that Freddie did not feel a little uneasy as the result of this scene would be untrue. There had been something in the confident manner in which the other had spoken of revenging himself that he had not at all liked. The words had had a sinister ring, and all through the rest of the day he pondered thoughtfully, wondering what a man so trained in the art of having things up his sleeve might have up it now. It was in meditative mood that he dined, and only on the following morning did his equanimity return to him.

Able, now that he had slept on it, to review the disturbing conversation in its proper perspective, he came to the conclusion that the fellow's threats had been mere bluff. What, after all, he asked himself, could this conjurer do? It was not as if they had been living in the Middle Ages, when chaps of that sort used to put spells on you and change you into things.

No, he decided, it was mere bluff, and with his complacency completely restored had just lighted a cigarette and fallen to dreaming of the girl he loved, when a telegram was brought to him.

It ran as follows:

Come at once. All lost. Ruin stares face. Love and kisses. Annabel.

Half an hour later he was in the train, speeding towards Droitgate Spa.

It had been Freddie's intention, on entering the train, to devote the journey to earnest meditation. But, as always happens when one wishes to concentrate and brood during a railway journey, he found himself closeted with a talkative fellow-traveller.

The one who interrupted Freddie's thoughts was a flabby, puffy man of middle age, wearing a red waistcoat, brown shoes, a morning coat and a bowler hat. With such a Grade A bounder, even had his mind been at rest, Freddie would have had little in common, and he sat chafing while the prismatic fellow prattled on. Nearly an hour passed before he was freed from the infliction of the other's conversation, but eventually the man's head began to nod, and presently he was snoring and Freddie was able to give himself up to his reverie.

His thoughts became less and less agreeable as the train rolled on. And what rendered his mental distress so particularly acute was the lack of detail in Annabel's telegram. It seemed to him to offer so wide a field for uncomfortable speculation.

"All lost," for instance. A man could do a lot of thinking about a phrase like that. And "Ruin stares face." Why, he asked himself, did ruin stare face? While commending Annabel's thriftiness in keeping the thing down to twelve words, he could not help wishing that she could have brought herself to spring another twopence and be more lucid.

But of one thing he felt certain. All this had something to do with his recent visitor. Behind that mystic telegram he seemed to see the hand of Mortimer Rackstraw, that hand whose quickness deceived the eye, and he knew that in lightly dismissing the other as a negligible force he had been too sanguine.

By the time he reached Podagra Lodge, the nervous strain had become almost intolerable. As he rang the bell he was quivering like some jelly set before a diet-patient, and the sight of Annabel's face as she opened the door did nothing to alleviate his perturbation. The girl was obviously all of a twitter.

"Oh, Freddie!" she cried. "The worst has happened."

Freddie gulped.

"Rackstraw?"

"Yes," said Annabel. "But how did you know
about him?"

"He came to see me, bubbling over a good deal with
veiled menaces and what not," explained Freddie.
He frowned, and eyed her closely. "Why didn't you
tell me you had been engaged to that bird?"

"I didn't think you would be interested. It was
just a passing girlish fancy."

"You're sure? You didn't really love this blighted
prestidigitator?"

"No, no. I was dazzled for a while, as any girl
might have been, when he sawed me in half, but then
you came along and I saw that I had been mistaken,
and that you were the only man in the world for me."

"Good egg," said Freddie, relieved.

He kissed her fondly and, as he did so, there came
to his ears the sound of rhythmic hammering from
somewhere below.

"What's that?" he asked.

Annabel wrung her hands.

"It's Mortimer!"

"Is he here?"

"Yes. He arrived on the one-fifteen. I locked
him in the cellar."

"Why?"

"To stop him going to the Pump Room."

"Why shouldn't he go to the Pump Room?"

M

"Because Sir Aylmer has gone there to listen to the band, and they must not meet. If they do, we are lost. Mortimer has hatched a fearful plot."

Freddie's heart seemed to buckle under within him. He had tried to be optimistic, but all along he had known that Mortimer Rackstraw would hatch some fearful plot. He could have put his shirt on it. A born hatcher.

"What plot?"

Annabel wrung her hands again.

"He means to introduce Sir Aylmer to my Uncle Joe. He wired to Uncle Joe to come to Droitgate Spa. He had arranged to meet him at the Pump Room, and then he was going to introduce him to Sir Aylmer."

Freddie was a little fogged. It did not seem to him much of a plot.

"Now that I can never be his, all he wants is to make himself unpleasant and prevent our marriage. And he knows that Sir Aylmer will never consent to your marrying me if he finds out that I have an uncle like Uncle Joe."

Freddie ceased to be fogged. He saw the whole devilish scheme now—a scheme worthy of the subtle brain that could put the ace of spades back in the pack, shuffle, cut three times, and then produce it from the inside of a lemon.

"Is he so frightful?" he quavered.

"Look," said Annabel simply. She took a photograph from her bosom and extended it towards him with a trembling hand. "That is Uncle Joe, taken in the lodge regalia of a Grand Exalted Periwinkle of the Mystic Order of Whelks."

Freddie glanced at the photograph and started back with a hoarse cry. Annabel nodded sadly.

"Yes," she said. "That is how he takes most people. The only faint hope I have is that he won't have been able to come. But if he has——"

"He has," cried Freddie, who had been fighting for breath. "We travelled down in the train together."

"What?"

"Yes. He must be waiting at the Pump Room now."

"And at any moment Mortimer will break his way out of the cellar. The door is not strong. What shall we do?"

"There is only one thing to do. I have all the papers . . ."

"You have no time to read now."

"The legal papers, the ones my uncle has to sign in order to release my money. There is just a chance that if I rush to the Pump Room I may get him to put his name on the dotted line before the worst happens."

"Then rush," cried Annabel.

"I will," said Freddie.

He kissed her quickly, grabbed his hat, and was off the mark like a jack rabbit.

A man who is endeavouring to lower the record for the distance between Podagra Lodge, which is in Arterio-Sclerosis Avenue, and the Droitgate Spa Pump Room has little leisure for thinking, but Freddie

managed to put in a certain amount as his feet skimmed
the pavement. And the trend of his thought such as
to give renewed vigour to his legs. He could scarcely
have moved more rapidly if he had been a character in
a two-reel film with the police after him.

And there was need for speed. Beyond a question,
Annabel had been right when she had said that Sir
Alymer would never consent to their union if he found
out that she had an uncle like her Uncle Joe. Uncle
Joe would get right in amongst him. Let them but
meet, and nothing was more certain than that the
haughty old man would veto the proposed nuptials.

A final burst of speed took him panting up the
Pump Room steps and into the rotunda where all that
was best and most refined in Droitgate Spa was
accustomed to assemble of an afternoon and listen to
the band. He saw Sir Aylmer in a distant seat and
hurried towards him.

"Gaw!" said Sir Aylmer. "You?"

Freddie could only nod.

"Well, stop puffing like that and sit down," said
Sir Aylmer. "They're just going to play 'Poet and
Peasant.'"

Freddie recovered his breath.

"Uncle," he began. But it was too late. Even as
he spoke, the conductor's baton fell and Sir Aylmer's
face assumed that reverent, doughlike expression of
attention so familiar in the rotundas of cure resorts.

"S'h," he said.

Of all the uncounted millions who in their time have
listened to bands playing "Poet and Peasant," few can

ever have listened with such a restless impatience as did
Frederick Fitch-Fitch on this occasion. Time was
flying. Every second was precious. At any moment
disaster might befall. And the band went on playing
as if it had taken on a life-job. It seemed to him an
eternity before the final oom-pom-pa.

"Uncle," he cried, as the echoes died away.

"S'h," said Sir Aylmer testily, and Freddie, with a
dull despair, perceived that they were going to get
an encore.

Of all the far-flung myriads who year in and year out
have listened to bands playing the overture to "Raymond," few can ever have chafed as did Frederick
Fitch-Fitch now. This suspense was unmanning him,
this delay was torture. He took the papers and a
fountain-pen from his pocket and toyed with them
nervously. He wondered dully as he sat there how the
opera "Raymond" had ever managed to get itself
performed, if the overture was as long as this. They
must have rushed it through in the last five minutes of
the evening as the audience groped for its hats and
wraps.

But there is an end to all things, even to the overture
from "Raymond." Just as the weariest river winds
somewhere safe to sea, so does this overture eventually
finish. And when it did, when the last notes faded
into silence and the conductor stood bowing and
smiling with that cool assumption, common to all
conductors, that it is they and not the perspiring
orchestra who have been doing the work, he started
again.

"Uncle," he said, "may I trouble you for a moment? . . . These papers."

Sir Aylmer cocked an eye at the documents.

"What papers are those?"

"The ones you have to sign, releasing my capital."

"Oh, those," said Sir Aylmer genially. The music had plainly mellowed him. "Of course, yes. Certainly, certainly. Give me . . ."

He broke off, and Freddie saw that he was looking at a distinguished, silvery-haired man with thin, refined features, who was sauntering by.

"Afternoon, Rumbelow," he said.

There was an unmistakable note of obsequiousness in Sir Aylmer's voice. His voice had become pink, and he was shuffling his feet and twiddling his fingers. The man to whom he had spoken paused and looked down. Seeing who it was that accosted him, he raised a silvery eyebrow. His manner was undisguisedly supercilious.

"Ah, Bastable," he said distantly.

A duller man than Sir Aylmer Bastable could not have failed to detect the cold hauteur in his voice. Freddie saw the flush on his uncle's face deepen. Sir Aylmer mumbled something about hoping that the distinguished-looking man was feeling better to-day.

"Worse," replied the other curtly. "Much worse. The doctors are baffled. Mine is a very complicated case." He paused for a moment, and his delicately chiselled lip curled in a sneer. "And how is the gout, Bastable? Gout! Ha, ha!"

Without waiting for a reply, he passed on and

joined a group that stood chatting close by. Sir
Aylmer choked down a mortified oath.

"Snob!" he muttered. "Thinks he's everybody
just because he's got telangiectasis. I don't see
what's so wonderful about having telangiectasis.
Anybody could have . . . What on earth are you
doing? What the devil's all this you're waving under
my nose? Papers? Papers? I don't want any
papers. Take them away, sir!"

And before Freddie could burst into the impassioned
plea which trembled on his lips, a commotion in the
doorway distracted his attention. His heart missed
a beat, and he sat there, frozen.

On the threshold stood Mortimer Rackstraw. He
was making some inquiry of an attendant, and Freddie
could guess only too well what that inquiry was.
Mortimer Rackstraw was asking which of those
present was Major-General Sir Aylmer Bastable.
Attached to his arm, obviously pleading with him and
appealing to his better self, Annabel Purvis gazed up
into his face with tear-filled eyes.

A moment later, the conjurer strode up, still towing
the girl. He halted before Sir Aylmer and threw
Annabel aside like a soiled glove. His face was cold
and hard and remorseless. With one hand he was
juggling mechanically with two billiard balls and a
bouquet of roses.

"Sir Aylmer Bastable?"

"Yes."

"I forbid the banns."

"What banns?"

"Their banns," said Mortimer Rackstraw, removing from his lips the hand with which he had been coldly curling his moustache and jerking it in the direction of Annabel and Freddie, who stood clasped in each other's arms, waiting for they knew not what.

"They're not up yet," said Annabel.

The conjurer seemed a little taken aback.

"Oh?" he said. "Well, when they are, I forbid them. And so will you, Sir Aylmer, when you hear all."

Sir Aylmer puffed.

"Who is this tight bounder?" he asked irritably.

Mortimer Rackstraw shook his head and took the two of clubs from it.

"A bounder, maybe," he said, "but not tight. I have come here, Sir Aylmer, in a spirit of altruism to warn you that if you allow your nephew to marry this girl the grand old name of Bastable will be mud."

Sir Aylmer started.

"Mud?"

"Mud. She comes from the very dregs of society."

"I don't," cried Annabel.

"Of course she doesn't," cried Freddie.

"Certainly she does not," assented Sir Aylmer warmly. "She told me herself that her father was a colonel."

Mortimer Rackstraw uttered a short, sneering laugh and took an egg from his left elbow.

"She did, eh? Did she add that he was a colonel in the Salvation Army?"

"What!"

"And that before he saw the light he was a Silver

Ring bookie, known to all the heads as Rat-Faced Rupert, the Bermondsey Twister?"

"Good God!"

Sir Aylmer turned to the girl with an awful frown. "Is this true?"

"Of course it's true," said Mortimer Rackstraw. "And if you want further proof of her unfitness to be your nephew's bride, just take a look at her Uncle Joe, who is now entering left-centre."

And Freddie, listless now and without hope, saw that his companion of the train was advancing towards them. He heard Sir Aylmer gasp and was aware that Annabel had stiffened in his arms. He was not surprised. The sun, filtering through the glass of the rotunda, lit up the man's flabby puffiness, his morning coat, his red waistcoat and his brown shoes, and rarely if ever, thought Freddie, could the sun of Droitgate Spa have shone on a more ghastly outsider.

There was nothing, however, in the newcomer's demeanour to suggest that he felt himself out of place in these refined surroundings His manner had an easy self-confidence. He sauntered up and without *gêne* slapped the conjurer on the back and patted Annabel on the shoulder.

"'Ullo, Mort. 'Ullo, Annie, my dear."

Sir Aylmer, who had blinked, staggered and finally recovered himself, spoke in a voice of thunder.

"You, sir! Is this true?"

"What's that, old cock?"

"Are you this girl's uncle?"

"That's right."

"Gaw!" said Sir Aylmer.

He would have spoken further, but at this point the band burst into "Pomp and Circumstance," and conversation was temporarily suspended. When it became possible once more for the human voice to make itself heard, it was Annabel's Uncle Joe who took the floor. He had recognized Freddie.

"Why, I've met you," he said. "We travelled down in the train together. Who's this young feller, Annie, that's huggin' and squeezin' you?"

"He is the man I am going to marry," said Annabel.

"He is not the man you are going to marry," said Sir Aylmer.

"Yes, I am the man she is going to marry," said Freddie.

"No, you're not the man she is going to marry," said Mortimer Rackstraw.

Annabel's Uncle Joe seemed puzzled. He appeared not to know what to make of this conflict of opinion.

"Well, settle it among yourselves," he said genially. "All I know is that whoever does marry you, Annie, is going to get a good wife."

"That's me," said Freddie.

"No, it isn't," said Sir Aylmer.

"Yes, it is," said Annabel.

"No, it's not," said Mortimer Rackstraw.

"Because I'm sure no man," proceeded Uncle Joe, "ever had a better niece. I've never forgotten the way you used to come and smooth my pillow and bring me cooling drinks when I was in the hospital."

There was the sound of a sharp intake of breath.

Sir Aylmer, who was saying, "It isn't, it isn't, it isn't," had broken off abruptly.

"Hospital?" he said. "Were you ever in a hospital?"

Mr. Boffin laughed indulgently.

"Was I ever in a hospital! That's a good 'un. That would make the boys on the Medical Council giggle. Ask them at St. Luke's if Joe Boffin was ever in a hospital. Ask them at St. Christopher's. Why, I've spent most of my life in hospitals. Started as a child with Congenital Pyloric Hypertrophy of the Stomach and never looked back."

Sir Aylmer was trembling violently. A look of awe had come into his face, the look which a small boy wears when he sees a heavyweight champion of the world.

"Did you say your name was Joe Boffin?"

"That's right."

"Not *the* Joe Boffin? Not the man there was that interview with in the Christmas number of *The Lancet*?"

"That's me."

Sir Aylmer started forward impulsively.

"May I shake your hand?"

"Put it there."

"I am proud to meet you, Mr. Boffin. I am one of your greatest admirers."

"Nice of you to say so, ol' man."

"Your career has been an inspiration to me. Is it really true that you have Thrombosis of the Heart *and* Vesicular Emphysema of the Lungs?"

"That's right."

"And that your temperature once went up to 107.5?"

"Twice. When I had Hyperpyrexia."

Sir Aylmer sighed.

"The best I've ever done is 102.2."

Joe Boffin patted him on the back.

"Well, that's not bad," he said. "Not bad at all."

"Excuse me," said a well-bred voice.

It was the distinguished-looking man with the silvery hair who had approached them, the man Sir Aylmer had addressed as Rumbelow. His manner was diffident. Behind him stood an eager group, staring and twiddling their fingers.

"Excuse me, my dear Bastable, for intruding on a private conversation, but I fancied . . . and my friends fancied . . ."

"We all fancied," said the group.

"That we overheard the name Boffin. Can it be, sir, that you are Mr. *Joseph* Boffin?"

"That's right."

"Boffin of St. Luke's?"

"That's right."

The silvery-haired man seemed overcome by a sudden shyness. He giggled nervously.

"Then may we say—my friends and I—how much . . . We felt we would just like . . . Unwarrantable intrusion, of course, but we are all such great admirers. I suppose you have to go through a good deal of this sort of thing, Mr. Boffin. . . . People coming up to you, I mean, and . . . Perfect strangers, I mean to say . . ."

"Quite all right, old man, quite all right.   Always glad to meet the fans."

"Then may I introduce myself.   I am Lord Rumbelow.   These are my friends, the Duke of Mull, the Marquis of Peckham, Lord Percy . . ."

"'Ow are you, 'ow are you?   Come and join us, boys.   My niece, Miss Purvis."

"Charmed."

"The young chap she's going to marry."

"How do you do?"

"And his uncle, Sir Aylmer Bastable."

All heads were turned towards the Major-General. Lord Rumbelow spoke in awed voice.

"Is this really so, Bastable?   Your nephew is actually going to marry Mr. Boffin's niece?   I congratulate you, my dear fellow.   A most signal honour." A touch of embarrassment came into his manner.   He coughed.   "We were just talking about you, oddly enough, Bastable, my friends and I.   Saying what a pity it was that we saw so little of you.   And we were wondering—it was the Duke's suggestion —if you would care to become a member of a little club we have—quite a small affair—rather exclusive, we like to feel—the Twelve Jolly Stretcher-Cases. . . ."

"My dear Rumbelow!"

"We have felt for a long time that our company was incomplete without you.   So you will join us? Capital, capital!   Perhaps you will look in there to-night?   Mr. Boffin, of course," he went on deprecatingly, "would, I am afraid, hardly condescend to

allow himself to be entertained by so humble a little
circle.   Otherwise——"

Joe Boffin slapped him affably on the back.

"My dear feller, I'd be delighted.   There's nothing
stuck-up about me."

"Well, really!   I hardly know what to say. . . ."

"We can't all be Joe Boffins.   That's the way I
look at it."

"The true democratic spirit."

"Why, I was best man at a chap's wedding last
week, and all he'd got was emotional dermatitis."

"Amazing!   Then you and Sir Aylmer will be with
us to-night?   Delightful.   We can give you a bottle
of lung tonic which I think you will appreciate.   We
pride ourselves on our cellar."

A babble of happy chatter had broken out, almost
drowning the band, and Mr. Boffin, opening his waistcoat, was showing the Duke of Mull the scar left by
his first operation.   Sir Aylmer, watching them with
throbbing heart, was dizzily aware of a fountain-pen
being thrust into his hand.

"Eh?" he said.   "What? What's this?   What,
what?"

"The papers," said Freddie.   "The merry old
documents in the case.   You sign here, where my
thumb is."

"Eh?   What?   Eh?   Ah, yes, to be sure.   Yes,
yes, yes," said Sir Aylmer, absently affixing his
signature.

"Thank you, uncle, a thousand . . ."

"Quite, quite.   But don't bother me now, my

boy. Busy. Got a lot to talk about to those friends of mine. Take the girl away and give her a sulphur water."

And, brushing aside Mortimer Rackstraw, who was offering him a pack of cards, he joined the group about Joe Boffin. Freddie clasped Annabel in a fond embrace. Mortimer Rackstraw stood glaring for a moment, twisting his moustache. Then he took the flags of all nations from Annabel's back hair and, with a despairing gesture, strode from the room.

A BIT OF LUCK FOR MABEL

"Get on with it."

"In my case it was a top-hat."

"What was a top-hat?"

"The snag."

"You stubbed your toe on a top-hat?"

"Figuratively, yes. It was a top-hat which altered the whole course of my life."

"You never had a top-hat."

"Yes, I did have a top-hat. It's absurd for you to pretend that I never had a top-hat. You know perfectly well that when I go to live with my Aunt Julia in Wimbledon I roll in top-hats—literally roll."

"Oh, yes, when you go to live with your aunt."

"Well, it was when I was living with her that I met Mabel. The affair of the top-hat happened——"

I looked at my watch again.

"I can give you half an hour," I said. "After that I'm going to bed. If you can condense Mabel into a thirty-minute sketch, carry on."

"This is not quite the sympathetic attitude I should like to see in an old friend, Corky."

"It's the only attitude I'm capable of at half-past three in the morning. Snap into it."

Ukridge pondered.

"It's difficult to know where to begin."

"Well, to start with, who was she?"

"She was the daughter of a bloke who ran some sort of immensely wealthy business in Singapore."

"Where did she live?"

"In Onslow Square."

"Where were you living?"

"With my aunt in Wimbledon."

"Where did you meet her?"

"At a dinner-party at my aunt's."

"You fell in love with her at first sight?"

"Yes."

"For a while it seemed that she might return your love?"

"Exactly."

"And then one day she saw you in a top-hat and the whole thing was off. There you are. The entire story in two minutes fifteen seconds. Now let's go to bed."

Ukridge shook his head.

"You've got it wrong, old horse. Nothing like that at all. You'd better let me tell the whole thing from the beginning."

The first thing I did after that dinner (said Ukridge) was to go and call at Onslow Square. As a matter of fact, I called about three times in the first week; and it seemed to me that everything was going like a breeze. You know what I'm like when I'm staying with my Aunt Julia, Corky. Dapper is the word. Debonair. Perfectly groomed. Mind you, I don't say I enjoy dressing the way she makes me dress when I'm with her, but there's no getting away from it that it gives me an air. Seeing me strolling along the street with the gloves, the cane, the spats, the shoes, and the old top-hat, you might wonder if I

was a marquess or a duke, but you would be pretty
sure I was one of the two.

These things count with a girl. They count still
more with her mother. By the end of the second
week you wouldn't be far wrong in saying that I was
the popular pet at Onslow Square. And then, rolling
in one afternoon for a dish of tea, I was shocked to
perceive nestling in my favourite chair, with all the
appearance of a cove who is absolutely at home,
another bloke. Mabel's mother was fussing over
him as if he were the long-lost son. Mabel seemed to
like him a good deal. And the nastiest shock of all
came when I discovered that the fellow was a baronet.

Now, you know as well as I do, Corky, that for the
ordinary workaday bloke Barts are tough birds to
go up against. There is something about Barts that
appeals to the most soulful girl. And as for the
average mother, she eats them alive. Even an elderly
Bart with two chins and a bald head is bad enough,
and this was a young and juicy specimen. He had a
clean-cut, slightly pimply, patrician face; and, what
was worse, he was in the Coldstream Guards. And
you will bear me out, Corky, when I say that, while
an ordinary civilian Bart is bad enough, a Bart who is
also a Guardee is a rival the stoutest-hearted cove
might well shudder at.

And when you consider that practically all I had to
put up against this serious menace was honest worth
and a happy disposition, you will understand why the
brow was a good deal wrinkled as I sat sipping my
tea and listening to the rest of the company talking

about people I'd never heard of and entertainments
where I hadn't been among those we also noticed.

After a while the conversation turned to Ascot.

"Are you going to Ascot, Mr. Ukridge?" said Mabel's
mother, apparently feeling that it was time to include
me in the chit-chat.

"Wouldn't miss it for worlds," I said.

Though, as a matter of fact, until that moment I
had rather intended to give it the go-by. Fond as I
am of the sport of kings, to my mind a race meeting
where you've got to go in a morning coat and a top-
hat—with the thermometer probably in the nineties
—lacks fascination. I'm all for being the young
duke when occasion requires, but races and toppers
don't seem to me to go together.

"That's splendid," said Mabel, and I'm bound to
say these kind words cheered me up a good deal.
"We shall meet there."

"Sir Aubrey," said Mabel's mother, "has invited us
to his house-party."

"Taken a place for the week down there," explained
the Bart.

"Ah!" I said. And, mark you, that was about all
there was to say. For the sickening realization that
this Guardee Bart, in addition to being a Bart and a
Guardee, also possessed enough cash to take country
houses for Ascot Week in that careless, off-hand manner
seemed to go all over me like nettle-rash. I was
rattled, Corky. Your old friend was rattled. I did
some pretty tense thinking on my way back to
Wimbledon.

When I got there, I found my aunt in the drawing-room.   And suddenly something in her attitude seemed to smite me like a blow.   I don't know if you have ever had that rummy feeling which seems to whisper in your ear that Hell's foundations are about to quiver, but I got it the moment I caught sight of her.   She was sitting bolt upright in a chair, and as I came in she looked at me.   You know her, Corky, and you know just how she shoots her eyes at you without turning her head, as if she were a basilisk with a stiff neck.   Well, that's how she looked at me now.

"Good evening," she said.

"Good evening," I said.

"So you've come in," she said.

"Yes," I said.

"Well, then, you can go straight out again," she said.

"Eh," I said.

"And never come back," she said.

I goggled at her.   Mark you, I had been heaved out of the old home by my Aunt Julia many a time before, so it wasn't as if I wasn't used to it; but I had never got the boot quite so suddenly before and so completely out of a blue sky.   Usually, when Aunt Julia bungs me out on my ear, it is possible to see it coming days ahead.

"I might have guessed that something like this would happen," she said.

And then all things were made plain.   She had found out about the clock.   And it shows what love

can do to a fellow, Corky, when I tell you that I
had clean forgotten all about it.

You know the position of affairs when I go to live
with my Aunt Julia. She feeds me and buys me
clothes, but for some reason best known to her own
distorted mind it is impossible to induce her to part
with a little ready cash. The consequence was that,
falling in love with Mabel as I had done and needing
a quid or two for current expenses, I had had to rely
on my native ingenuity and resource. It was absolutely imperative that I should give the girl a few
flowers and chocolates from time to time, and this
runs into money. So, seeing a rather juicy clock
doing nothing on the mantelpiece of the spare bedroom, I had sneaked it off under my coat and put
it up the spout at the local pawnbroker's. And now,
apparently, in some devious and underhand manner
she had discovered this.

Well, it was no good arguing. When my Aunt
Julia is standing over you with her sleeves rolled up
preparatory to getting a grip on the scruff of your
neck and the seat of your trousers, it has always been
my experience that words are useless. The only
thing to do is to drift away and trust to Time, the
great healer. Some forty minutes later, therefore,
a solitary figure might have been observed legging it
to the station with a suit-case. I was out in the great
world once more.

However, you know me, Corky. The Old Campaigner. It takes more than a knock like that to

crush your old friend. I took a bed-sitting-room in Arundel Street and sat down to envisage the situation.

Undeniably things had taken a nasty twist, and many a man lacking my vision and enterprise might have turned his face to the wall and said: "This is the end!" But I am made of sterner stuff. It seemed to me that all was not yet over. I had packed the morning coat, the waistcoat, the trousers, the shoes, the spats, and the gloves, and had gone away wearing the old top-hat; so, from a purely ornamental point of view, I was in precisely the position I had been before. That is to say, I could still continue to call at Onslow Square; and, what is more, if I could touch George Tupper for a fiver—which I intended to do without delay—I should have the funds to go to Ascot.

The sun, it appeared to me, therefore, was still shining. How true it is, Corky, that, no matter how the tempests lower, there is always sunshine somewhere! How true it is—Oh, all right, I was only mentioning it.

Well, George Tupper, splendid fellow, parted without a murmur. Well, no, not—to be absolutely accurate—without a murmur. Still, he parted. And the position of affairs was now as follows. Cash in hand, five pounds. Price of admission to grandstand and paddock at Ascot for first day of meeting, two pounds. Time to elapse before Ascot, ten days. Net result—three quid in my kick to keep me going till then and pay my fare down and buy flowers and so on. It all looked very rosy.

But note, Corky, how Fate plays with us. Two days before Ascot, as I was coming back from having tea at Onslow Square—not a little preoccupied, for the Bart had been very strong on the wing that afternoon—there happened what seemed at first sight an irremediable disaster.

The weather, which had been fair and warm until that evening, had suddenly broken, and a rather nippy wind had sprung up from the east. Now, if I had not been so tensely occupied with my thoughts, brooding on the Bart, I should of course have exercised reasonable precautions; but, as it was, I turned the corner into the Fulham Road in what you might call a brown study; and the first thing I knew my top-hat had been whisked off my head and was tooling along briskly in the direction of Putney.

Well, you know what the Fulham Road's like. A top-hat has about as much chance in it as a rabbit at a dog-show. I dashed after the thing with all possible speed, but what was the use? A taxi-cab knocked it sideways towards a 'bus; and the 'bus, curse it, did the rest. By the time the traffic had cleared a bit, I caught sight of the ruins and turned away with a silent groan. The thing wasn't worth picking up.

So there I was, dished.

Or, rather, what the casual observer who didn't know my enterprise and resource would have called dished. For a man like me, Corky, may be down, but he is never out. So swift were my mental processes that the time that elapsed between the sight of that ruined hat and my decision to pop round to

the Foreign Office and touch George Tupper for
another fiver was not more than fifty seconds. It is
in the crises of life that brains really tell.

You can't accumulate if you don't speculate. So,
though funds were running a bit low by this time, I
invested a couple of bob in a cab. It was better to
be two shillings out than to risk getting to the Foreign
Office and finding that Tuppy had left.

Well, late though it was, he was still there. That's
one of the things I like about George Tupper, one of
the reasons why I always maintain that he will rise
to impressive heights in his country's service—he
does not shirk; he is not a clock-watcher. Many
civil servants are apt to call it a day at five o'clock,
but not George Tupper. That is why one of these
days, Corky, when you are still struggling along
turning out articles for *Interesting Bits* and writing
footling short stories about girls who turn out to
be the missing heiress, Tuppy will be Sir George
Tupper, K.C.M.G., and a devil of a fellow among the
Chancelleries.

I found him up to his eyes in official-looking
papers, and I came to the point with all speed. I
knew that he was probably busy declaring war on
Montenegro or somewhere and wouldn't want a lot of
idle chatter.

"Tuppy, old horse," I said, "it is imperative that I
have a fiver immediately."

"A what?" said Tuppy.

"A tenner," I said.

It was at this point that I was horrified to observe

in the man's eye that rather cold, forbidding look
which you sometimes see in blokes' eyes on these
occasions.

"I lent you five pounds only a week ago," he
said.

"And may Heaven reward you, old horse," I replied,
courteously.

"What do you want any more for?"

I was just about to tell him the whole circumstances
when it was as if a voice whispered to me: "Don't do
it!" Something told me that Tuppy was in a nasty
frame of mind and was going to turn me down—yes,
me, an old schoolfellow, who had known him since he
was in Eton collars. And at the same time I suddenly
perceived, lying on a chair by the door, Tuppy's
topper. For Tuppy is not one of those civil servants
who lounge into Whitehall in flannels and a straw
hat. He is a correct dresser, and I honour him for it.

"What on earth," said Tuppy, "do you need money
for?"

"Personal expenses, laddie," I replied. "The cost
of living is very high these days."

"What you want," said Tuppy, "is work."

"What I want," I reminded him—if old Tuppy has
a fault, it is that he will not stick to the point—"is a
fiver."

He shook his head in a way I did not like to
see.

"It's very bad for you, all this messing about on
borrowed money. It's not that I grudge it to you,"
said Tuppy; and I knew, when I heard him talk in that

pompous, Foreign Official way, that something had
gone wrong that day in the country's service. Probably the draft treaty with Switzerland had been
pinched by a foreign adventuress. That sort of thing
is happening all the time in the Foreign Office. Mysterious veiled women blow in on old Tuppy and engage
him in conversation, and when he turns round he
finds the long blue envelope with the important papers
in it gone.

"It's not that I grudge you the money," said
Tuppy, "but you really ought to be in some regular
job. I must think," said Tuppy, "I must think. I
must have a look round."

"And meanwhile," I said, "the fiver?"

"No. I'm not going to give it to you."

"Only five pounds," I urged. "Five little pounds,
Tuppy, old horse."

"No."

"You can chalk it up in the books to Office Expenses
and throw the burden on the taxpayer."

"No."

"Will nothing move you?"

"No. And I'm awfully sorry, old man, but I must
ask you to clear out now. I'm terribly busy."

"Oh, right-ho," I said.

He burrowed down into the documents again; and
I moved to the door, scooped up the top-hat from the
chair, and passed out.

Next morning, when I was having a bit of breakfast,
in rolled old Tuppy.

"I say," said Tuppy.

"Say on, laddie."

"You know when you came to see me yesterday?"

"Yes. You've come to tell me you've changed your mind about that fiver?"

"No, I haven't come to tell you I've changed my mind about that fiver. I was going to say that, when I started to leave the office, I found my top-hat had gone."

"Too bad," I said.

Tuppy gave me a piercing glance.

"You didn't take it, I suppose?"

"Who, me? What would I want with a top-hat?"

"Well, it's very mysterious."

"I expect you'll find it was pinched by an international spy or something."

Tuppy brooded for some moments.

"It's all very odd," he said. "I've never had it happen to me before."

"One gets new experiences."

"Well, never mind about that. What I really came about was to tell you that I think I have got you a job."

"You don't mean that!"

"I met a man at the club last night who wants a secretary. It's more a matter with him of having somebody to keep his papers in order and all that sort of thing, so typing and shorthand are not essential. You can't do shorthand, I suppose?"

"I don't know. I've never tried."

"Well, you're to go and see him to-morrow morning at ten. His name's Bulstrode, and you'll find him at

my club. It's a good chance, so for Heaven's sake
don't be lounging in bed at ten."

"I won't. I'll be up and ready, with a heart for
any fate."

"Well, mind you are."

"And I am deeply grateful, Tuppy, old horse, for
these esteemed favours."

"That's all right," said Tuppy. He paused at the
door. "It's a mystery about that hat."

"Insoluble, I should say. I shouldn't worry any
more about it."

"One moment it was there, and the next it had gone."

"How like life!" I said. "Makes one think a bit,
that sort of thing."

He pushed off, and I was just finishing my breakfast
when Mrs. Beale, my landlady, came in with a letter.

It was from Mabel, reminding me to be sure to come
to Ascot. I read it three times while I was consuming
a fried egg; and I am not ashamed to say, Corky, that
tears filled my eyes. To think of her caring so much
that she should send special letters urging me to be
there made me tremble like a leaf. It looked to me as
though the Bart's number was up. Yes, at that
moment, Corky, I felt positively sorry for the Bart,
who was in his way quite a good chap, though pimply.

That night I made my final preparations. I counted
the cash in hand. I had just enough to pay my fare to
Ascot and back, my entrance fee to the grandstand and
paddock, with a matter of fifteen bob over for lunch
and general expenses and a thoughtful ten bob to do
a bit of betting with. Financially, I was on velvet.

o

Nor was there much wrong with the costume depart-
ment. I dug out the trousers, the morning coat, the
waistcoat, the shoes and the spats, and I tried on
Tuppy's topper again. And for the twentieth time I
wished that old Tuppy, a man of sterling qualities in
every other respect, had had a slightly bigger head.
It's a curious thing about old George Tupper. There's
a man who you might say is practically directing
the destinies of a great nation—at any rate, he's in the
Foreign Office and extremely well thought of by
the Nibs—and yet his size in hats is a small seven. I
don't know if you've ever noticed that Tuppy's head
goes up to a sort of point. Mine, on the other hand,
is shaped more like a mangel-wurzel, and this made
the whole thing rather complex and unpleasant.

As I stood looking in the glass, giving myself a
final inspection, I couldn't help feeling what a difference a hat makes to a man. Bare-headed, I was
perfect in every detail; but with a hat on I looked a
good deal like a bloke about to go on and do a comic
song at one of the halls. Still, there it was, and it
was no good worrying about it. I put the trousers
under the mattress, to ensure an adequate crease;
and I rang the bell for Mrs. Beale and gave her the
coat to press with a hot iron. I also gave her the hat
and instructed her to rub stout on it. This, as you
doubtless know, gives a topper the deuce of a gloss;
and when a fellow is up against a Bart, he can't afford
to neglect the smallest detail.

And so to bed.

I didn't sleep very well. At about one in the

morning it started to rain in buckets, and the thought suddenly struck me: what the deuce was I going to do if it rained during the day? To buy an umbrella would simply dislocate the budget beyond repair. The consequence was that I tossed pretty restlessly on my pillow.

But all was well. When I woke at eight o'clock the sun was pouring into the room, and the last snag seemed to have been removed from my path. I had breakfast, and then I dug the trouserings out from under the mattress, slipped into them, put on the shoes, buckled the spats, and rang the bell for Mrs. Beale. I was feeling debonair to a degree. The crease in the trousers was perfect.

"Oh, Mrs. Beale," I said. "The coat and the hat, please. What a lovely morning!"

Now, this Beale woman, I must tell you, was a slightly sinister sort of female, with eyes that reminded me a good deal of my Aunt Julia. And I was now somewhat rattled to perceive that she was looking at me in a rather meaning kind of manner. I also perceived that she held in her hand a paper or document. And there shot through me, Corky, a nameless fear.

It's a kind of instinct, I suppose. A man who has been up against it as frequently as I have comes to shudder automatically when he sees a landlady holding a sheet of paper and looking at him in a meaning manner.

A moment later it was plain that my sixth sense had not deceived me.

"I've brought your little account, Mr. Ukridge,"
said this fearful female.

"Right!" I said, heartily. "Just shove it on the
table, will you? And bring the coat and hat."

She looked more like my Aunt Julia than ever.

"I must ask you for the money now," she said.
"Being a week overdue."

All this was taking the sunshine out of the morning,
but I remained debonair.

"Yes, yes," I said. "I quite understand. We'll
have a good long talk about that later. The hat and
coat, please, Mrs. Beale."

"I must ask you——" she was beginning again, but
I checked her with one of my looks. If there's one
thing I bar in this world, Corky, it's sordidness.

"Yes, yes," I said testily. "Some other time. I
want the hat and coat, please."

At this moment, by the greatest bad luck, her
vampire gaze fell on the mantelpiece. You know how
it is when you are dressing with unusual care—you fill
your pockets last thing. And I had most unfortunately
placed my little capital on the mantelpiece. Too late
I saw that she had spotted it. Take the advice of a
man who has seen something of life, Corky, and never
leave your money lying about. It's bound to start a
disagreeable train of thought in the mind of anyone
who sees it.

"You've got the money there," said Mrs. Beale.

I leaped for the mantelpiece and trousered the cash.

"No, no," I said, hastily. "You can't have that.
I need that."

"Ho?" she said. "So do I."

"Now listen, Mrs. Beale," I said. "You know as well as I do——"

"I know as well as you do that you owe me two pounds three and sixpence ha'penny."

"And in God's good time," I said, "you shall have it. But just for the moment you must be patient. Why, dash it, Mrs. Beale," I said, warmly, "you know as well as I do that in all financial transactions a certain amount of credit is an understood thing.   Credit is the life-blood of commerce. So bring the hat and coat, and later on we will thresh this matter out thoroughly."

And then this woman showed a baseness of soul, a horrible low cunning, which, I like to think, is rarely seen in the female sex.

"I'll either have the money," she said, "or I'll keep the coat and hat."   And words cannot express, Corky, the hideous malignity in her voice.   "They ought to fetch a bit."

I stared at her, appalled.

"But I can't go to Ascot without a top-hat."

"Then you'd better not go to Ascot."

"Be reasonable!" I begged.   "Reflect!"

It was no good.   She stood firm on her demand for two pounds three and sixpence ha'penny, and nothing that I could say would shift her.   I offered her double the sum at some future date, but no business was done. The curse of landladies as a class, Corky, and the reason why they never rise to ease and opulence, is that they have no vision.   They do not understand high finance.   They lack the big, broad, flexible outlook which wins to wealth. The deadlock continued, and finally she went off, leaving me dished once more.

It is only when you are in a situation like that, Corky, that you really begin to be able to appreciate the true hollowness of the world. It is only then that the absolute silliness and futility of human institutions comes home to you. This Ascot business, for instance. Why in the name of Heaven, if you are going to hold a race meeting, should you make a foolish regulation about the sort of costume people must wear if they want to attend it? Why should it be necessary to wear a top hat at Ascot, when you can go to all the other races in anything you like?

Here was I, perfectly equipped for Hurst Park, Sandown, Gatwick, Ally Pally, Lingfield, or any other meeting you care to name; and, simply because a ghoul of a landlady had pinched my topper, I was utterly debarred from going to Ascot, though the price of admission was bulging in my pocket. It's just that sort of thing that makes a fellow chafe at our modern civilization and wonder if, after all, Man can be Nature's last word.

Such, Corky, were my meditations as I stood at the window and gazed bleakly out at the sunshine. And then suddenly, as I gazed, I observed a bloke approaching up the street.

I eyed him with interest. He was an elderly, prosperous bloke with a yellowish face and a white moustache, and he was looking at the numbers on the doors, as if he were trying to spot a destination. And at this moment he halted outside the front door of my house, squinted up at the number, and then trotted up the steps and rang the bell. And I realized at once that this must be Tuppy's secretary man, the fellow I was due to go and see at the club in another half-hour. For a moment it seemed odd that he should have come to call on me instead of waiting for me to call on him; and then I reflected that this was just the sort of thing that the energetic, world's-worker type of man that Tuppy chummed up with at his club would be likely to do. Time is money with these coves, and no doubt he had remembered some other appointment which he couldn't make if he waited at his club till ten.

Anyway, here he was, and I peered down at him with a beating heart. For what sent a thrill through me, Corky, was the fact that he was much about my build and was brightly clad in correct morning costume with top-hat complete. And though it was hard to tell exactly at such a distance and elevation, the thought flashed across me like an inspiration from above that that top-hat would fit me a dashed sight better than Tuppy's had done.

In another minute there was a knock on the door, and he came in.

Seeing him at close range, I perceived that I had not misjudged this man. He was shortish, but his shoulders were just about the same size as mine, and his head was large and round. If ever, in a word, a bloke might have been designed by Providence to wear a coat and hat that would fit me, this bloke was that bloke. I gazed at him with a gleaming eye.

"Mr. Ukridge?"

"Yes," I said. "Come in. Awfully good of you to call."

"Not at all."

And now, Corky, as you will no doubt have divined, I was, so to speak, at the cross-roads. The finger-post of Prudence pointed one way, that of Love another. Prudence whispered to me to conciliate this bloke, to speak him fair, to comport myself towards him as towards one who held my destinies in his hand and who could, if well disposed, give me a job which would keep the wolf from the door while I was looking round for something bigger and more attuned to my vision and abilities.

Love, on the other hand, was shouting to me to pinch his coat and hat and leg it for the open spaces.

It was the deuce of a dilemma.

"I have called——" began the bloke.

I made up my mind. Love got the decision.

"I say," I said. "I think you've got something on the back of your coat."

"Eh?" said the bloke, trying to squint round and look between his shoulder-blades—silly ass.

"It's a squashed tomato or something."

"A squashed tomato?"

"Or something."

"How would I get a squashed tomato on my coat?"

"Ah!" I said, giving him to understand with a wave of the hand that these were deep matters.

"Very curious," said the bloke.

"Very," I said. "Slip off your coat and let's have a look at it."

He slid out of the coat, and I was on it like a knife. You have to move quick on these occasions, and I moved quick. I had the coat out of his hand and the top-hat off the table where he had put it, and was out of the door and dashing down the stairs before he could utter a yip.

I put on the coat, and it fitted like a glove. I slapped the top-hat on to my head, and it might have been made for me. And then I went out into the sunshine, as natty a specimen as ever paced down Piccadilly.

I was passing down the front steps when I heard a sort of bellow from above. There was the bloke, protruding from the window; and, strong man though I am, Corky, I admit that for an instant I quailed at the sight of the hideous fury that distorted his countenance.

"Come back!" shouted the bloke.

Well, it wasn't a time for standing and making explanations and generally exchanging idle chatter. When a man is leaning out of window in his shirt-sleeves, making the amount of noise that this cove was making, it doesn't take long for a crowd to gather. And my experience has been that, when a crowd gathers, it isn't much longer before some infernal, officious policeman rolls round as well. Nothing was farther from my wishes than to have this little purely private affair between the bloke and myself sifted by a policeman in front of a large crowd.

So I didn't linger. I waved my hand as much as to

say that all would come right in the future, and then I
nipped at a fairly high rate of speed round the corner
and hailed a taxi. It had been no part of my plans to
incur the expense of a taxi, I having ear-marked twopence for a ride on the Tube to Waterloo; but there are
times when economy is false prudence.

Once in the cab, whizzing along and putting more
distance between the bloke and myself with every
revolution of the wheels, I perked up amazingly. I
had been, I confess, a trifle apprehensive until now;
but from this moment everything seemed splendid.
I forgot to mention it before, but this final top-hat
which how nestled so snugly on the brow was a grey
top-hat; and, if there is one thing that really lends a
zip and a sort of devilish fascination to a fellow's
appearance, it is one of those grey toppers. As I
looked at myself in the glass and then gazed out of
window at the gay sunshine, it seemed to me that God
was in His Heaven and all was right with the world.

The general excellence of things continued. I had a
pleasant journey; and when I got to Ascot I planked
my ten bob on a horse I had heard some fellows talking
about in the train, and, by Jove, it ambled home at a
crisp ten to one. So there I was, five quid ahead of
the game almost, you might say, before I had got there.
It was with an uplifted heart, Corky, that I strolled off
to the paddock to have a look at the multitude and try
to find Mabel. And I had hardly emerged from that
tunnel thing that you have to walk through to get
from the stand to the paddock when I ran into old
Tuppy.

My first feeling on observing the dear old chap was
one of relief that I wasn't wearing his hat. Old Tuppy
is one of the best, but little things are apt to upset him,
and I was in no mood for a painful scene. I passed
the time of day genially.

"Ah, Tuppy!" I said.

George Tupper is a man with a heart of gold, but he
is deficient in tact.

"How the deuce did you get here?" he asked.

"In the ordinary way, laddie," I said.

"I mean, what are you doing here, dressed up to the
nines like this?"

"Naturally," I replied, with a touch of stiffness,
"when I come to Ascot, I wear the accepted morning
costume of the well-dressed Englishman."

"You look as if you had come into a fortune."

"Yes?" I said, rather wishing he would change the
subject. In spite of what you might call the perfect
alibi of the grey topper, I did not want to discuss hats
and clothes with Tuppy so soon after his recent bereave-
ment. I could see that the hat he had on was a brand-
new one and must have set him back at least a couple
of quid.

"I suppose you've gone back to your aunt?" said
Tuppy, jumping at a plausible solution. "Well, I'm
awfully glad, old man, because I'm afraid that secretary
job is off. I was going to write to you to-night."

"Off?" I said. Having had the advantage of seeing
the bloke's face as he hung out of window at the
moment of our parting, I knew it was off; but I couldn't
see how Tuppy could know.

"He rang me up last night, to tell me that he was afraid you wouldn't do, as he had thought it over and decided that he must have a secretary who knew shorthand."

"Oh?" I said. "Oh, did he? Then I'm dashed glad," I said, warmly, "that I pinched his hat. It will be a sharp lesson to him not to raise people's hopes and shilly-shally in this manner."

"Pinched his hat? What do you mean?"

I perceived that there was need for caution. Tuppy was looking at me in an odd manner, and I could see that the turn the conversation had taken was once more wakening in him suspicions which he ought to have known better than to entertain of an old school friend.

"It was like this, Tuppy," I said. "When you came to me and told me about that international spy sneaking your hat from the Foreign Office, it gave me an idea. I had been wanting to come to Ascot, but I had no topper. Of course, if I had pinched yours, as you imagined for a moment I had done, I should have had one; but, not having pinched yours, of course I hadn't one. So when your friend Bulstrode called on me this morning I collared his. And now that you have revealed to me what a fickle, changeable character he is, I'm very glad I did."

Tuppy gaped slightly.

"Bulstrode called on you this morning, did you say?"

"This morning at about half-past nine."

"He couldn't have done."

"Then how do you account for my having his hat? Pull yourself together, Tuppy, old horse."

"The man who came to see you couldn't have been Bulstrode."

"Why not?"

"He left for Paris last night."

"What!"

"He 'phoned me from the station just before his train started.   He had had to change his plans."

"Then who was the bloke?" I said.

The thing seemed to me to have the makings of one of those great historic mysteries you read about. I saw no reason why posterity should not discuss for ever the problem of the bloke in the grey topper as keenly as they do the man in the iron mask.   "The facts," I said, "are precisely as I have stated.   At nine-thirty this morning a bird, gaily apparrelled in morning coat, spongebag trousers, and grey top-hat, presented himself at my rooms and——"

At this moment a voice spoke behind me.

"Oh, hullo!"

I turned, and observed the Bart.

"Hullo!" I said.

I introduced Tuppy.   The Bart nodded courteously.

"I say," said the Bart.   "Where's the old man?"

"What old man?"

"Mabel's father.   Didn't he catch you?"

I stared at the man.   He appeared to me to be gibbering.   And a gibbering Bart is a nasty thing to have hanging about you before you have strengthened yourself with a bit of lunch.

"Mabel's father's in Singapore," I said.

"No, he isn't," said the Bart. "He got home yesterday, and Mabel sent him round to your place to pick you up and bring you down here in the car. Had you left before he arrived?"

Well, that's where the story ends, Corky. From the moment that pimply Baronet uttered those words, you might say that I faded out of the picture. I never went near Onslow Square again. Nobody can say that I lack nerve, but I hadn't nerve enough to creep into the family circle and resume acquaintance with that fearsome bloke. There are some men, no doubt, with whom I might have been able to pass the whole thing off with a light laugh, but that glimpse I had had of him as he bellowed out of the window told me that he was not one of them. I faded away, Corky, old horse, just faded away. And about a couple of months later I read in the paper that Mabel had married the Bart.

Ukridge sighed another sigh and heaved himself up from the sofa. Outside the world was blue-grey with the growing dawn, and even the later birds were busy among the worms.

"You might make a story out of that, Corky," said Ukridge.

"I might," I said.

"All profits to be shared on a strict fifty-fifty basis, of course."

"Of course."

Ukridge brooded.

"Though it really wants a bigger man to do it justice and tell it properly, bringing out all the fine

shades of the tragedy.   It wants somebody like Thomas
Hardy or Kipling, or somebody."

"Better let me have a shot at it."

"All right," said Ukridge.   "And, as regards a title,
I should call it 'His Lost Romance,' or something like
that.   Or would you suggest simply something terse
and telling, like 'Fate' or 'Destiny'?"

"I'll think of a title," I said.

BUTTERCUP DAY

BUTTERCUP DAY

"LADDIE," said Ukridge, "I need capital, old horse—need it sorely."

He removed his glistening silk hat, looked at it in a puzzled way, and replaced it on his head. We had met by chance near the eastern end of Piccadilly, and the breath-taking gorgeousness of his costume told me that, since I had seen him last, there must have occurred between him and his Aunt Julia one of those periodical reconciliations which were wont to punctuate his hectic and disreputable career. For those who know Stanley Featherstonehaugh Ukridge, that much-enduring man, are aware that he is the nephew of Miss Julia Ukridge, the wealthy and popular novelist, and that from time to time, when she can bring herself to forgive and let bygones be bygones, he goes to dwell for a while in gilded servitude at her house in Wimbledon.

"Yes, Corky, my boy, I want a bit of capital."

"Oh?"

"And want it quick. The truest saying in this world is that you can't accumulate if you don't speculate. But how the deuce are you to start speculating unless you accumulate a few quid to begin with?"

"Ah," I said, non-committally.

"Take my case," proceeded Ukridge, running a large, beautifully gloved finger round the inside of a spotless collar which appeared to fit a trifle too snugly to the neck. "I have an absolutely safe double for Kempton Park on the fifteenth, and even a modest investment would bring me in several hundred pounds. But bookies, blast them, require cash down in advance, so where am I? Without capital, enterprise is strangled at birth."

"Can't you get some from your aunt?"

"Not a cent. She is one of those women who simply do not disgorge. All her surplus cash is devoted to adding to her collection of mouldy snuff-boxes. When I look at those snuff-boxes and reflect that any single one of them, judiciously put up the spout, would set my feet on the road to Fortune, only my innate sense of honesty keeps me from pinching them."

"You mean they're locked up?"

"It's hard, laddie. Very hard and bitter and ironical. She buys me suits. She buys me hats. She buys me boots. She buys me spats. And, what is more, insists on my wearing the damned things. With what result? Not only am I infernally uncomfortable, but my exterior creates a totally false impression in the minds of any blokes I meet to whom I may happen to owe a bit of money. When I go about looking as if I owned the Mint, it becomes difficult to convince them that I am not in a position to pay them their beastly one pound fourteen and eleven, or whatever it is. I tell you, laddie, the strain has begun to weigh upon me to such an extent that the breaking-point may arrive at any moment. Every day it is becoming more imperative that I clear out and start life again upon my own. But this cannot be done without cash. And that is why I look around me and say to myself: 'How am I to acquire a bit of capital?'"

I thought it best to observe at this point that my own circumstances were extremely straitened. Ukridge received the information with a sad, indulgent smile.

"I was not dreaming of biting your ear, old horse," he said. "What I require is something far beyond your power to supply. Five pounds at least. Or three, anyway. Of course, if, before we part, you think fit to hand over a couple of bob or half-a-crown as a small temporary——"

He broke off with a start, and there came into his face the look of one who has perceived snakes in his path. He gazed along the street; then, wheeling round, hurried abruptly down Church Place.

"One of your creditors?" I asked.

"Girl with flags," said Ukridge, briefly. A peevish note crept into his voice. "This modern practice, laddie, of allowing females with trays of flags and collecting-boxes to flood the Metropolis is developing into a scourge. If it isn't Rose Day it's Daisy Day, and if it isn't Daisy Day it's Pansy Day. And though now, thanks to a bit of quick thinking, we have managed to escape without——"

At this moment a second flag-girl, emerging from Jermyn Street, held us up with a brilliant smile, and we gave till it hurt—which, in Ukridge's case, was almost immediately.

"And so it goes on," he said bitterly. "Sixpence here, a shilling there. Only last Friday I was touched for twopence at my very door. How can a man amass a huge fortune if there is this constant drain on his resources? What was that girl collecting for?"

"I didn't notice."

"Nor did I. One never does. For all we know, we may have contributed to some cause of which we heartily disapprove. And that reminds me, Corky, my aunt is lending her grounds on Tuesday for a bazaar in aid of the local Temperance League. I particularly wish you to put aside all other engagements and roll up."

"No, thanks. I don't want to meet your aunt again."

"You won't meet her. She will be away. She's going north on a lecturing tour."

"Well, I don't want to come to any bazaar. I can't afford it."

"Have no fear, laddie. There will be no expense involved. You will pass the entire afternoon in the house with me. My aunt, though she couldn't get out of lending these people her grounds, is scared that, with so many strangers prowling about, somebody might edge in and sneak her snuff-boxes. So I am left on guard, with instructions not to stir out till they've all gone. And a very wise precaution, too. There is absolutely nothing which blokes whose passions have been inflamed by constant ginger-beer will stick at. You will share my vigil. We will smoke a pipe or two in the study, talk of this and that, and it may be that, if we put our heads together, we shall be able to think up a scheme for collecting a bit of capital."

"Oh, well, in that case——"

"I shall rely on you. And now, if I don't want to be late, I'd better be getting along. I'm lunching with my aunt at Prince's."

He gazed malevolently at the flag-girl, who had just stopped another pedestrian, and strode off.

Heath House, Wimbledon, the residence of Miss Julia Ukridge, was one of that row of large mansions which face the Common, standing back from the road in the seclusion of spacious grounds. On any normal day, the prevailing note of the place would have been a dignified calm; but when I arrived on the Tuesday afternoon a vast and unusual activity was in progress. Over the gates there hung large banners advertising the bazaar, and through these gates crowds of people were passing. From somewhere in the interior of the garden came the brassy music of a merry-go-round. I added myself to the throng, and was making for the front door when a silvery voice spoke in my ear, and I was aware of a very pretty girl at my elbow.

"Buy a buttercup?"

"I beg your pardon?"

"Buy a buttercup?"

I then perceived that, attached to her person with a strap, she carried a tray containing a mass of yellow paper objects.

"What's all this?" I inquired, automatically feeling in my pocket.

She beamed upon me like a high priestess initiating some favourite novice into a rite.

"Buttercup Day," she said winningly.

A man of greater strength of mind would, no doubt, have asked what Buttercup Day was, but I have a spine of wax. I produced the first decent-sized coin on which my fumbling fingers rested, and slipped it into her box. She thanked me with a good deal of fervour and pinned one of the yellow objects in my buttonhole.

The interview then terminated. The girl flitted off like a sunbeam in the direction of a prosperous-looking man who had just gone by, and I went on to the house, where I found Ukridge in the study gazing earnestly through the French windows which commanded a view of the grounds. He turned as I entered; and, as his eye fell upon the saffron ornament in my coat, a soft smile of pleasure played about his mouth.

"I see you've got one," he said.

"Got what?"

"One of those thingummies."

"Oh, these? Yes. There was a girl with a tray of them in the front garden. It's Buttercup Day. In aid of something or other, I suppose."

"It's in aid of me," said Ukridge, the soft smile developing into a face-splitting grin.

"What do you mean?"

"Corky, old horse," said Ukridge, motioning me to

a chair, "the great thing in this world is to have a good, level business head. Many men in my position wanting capital and not seeing where they were going to get it, would have given up the struggle as a bad job. Why? Because they lacked Vision and the big, broad, flexible outlook. But what did I do? I sat down and thought. And after many hours of concentrated meditation I was rewarded with an idea. You remember that painful affair in Jermyn Street the other day—when that female bandit got into our ribs? You recall that neither of us knew what we had coughed up our good money for?"

"Well?"

"Well, laddie, it suddenly flashed upon me like an inspiration from above that nobody ever does know what they are coughing up for when they meet a girl with a tray of flags. I hit upon the great truth, old horse—one of the profoundest truths in this modern civilization of ours—that any given man, confronted by a pretty girl with a tray of flags, will automatically and without inquiry shove a coin in her box. So I got hold of a girl I know—a dear little soul, full of beans—and arranged for her to come here this afternoon. I confidently anticipate a clean-up on an impressive scale. The outlay on the pins and bits of paper was practically nil, so there is no overhead and all that comes in will be pure velvet."

A strong pang shot through me.

"Do you mean to say," I demanded with feeling, "that that half-crown of mine goes into your beastly pocket?"

"Half of it. Naturally my colleague and partner is in on the division. Did you really give half-a-crown?" said Ukridge, pleased. "It was like you, laddie. Generous to a fault. If everyone had your lavish disposition, this world would be a better, sweeter place."

"I suppose you realize," I said, "that in about ten minutes at the outside your colleague and partner, as you call her, will be arrested for obtaining money under false pretences?"

"Not a chance."

"After which, they will—thank God!—proceed to pinch you."

"Quite impossible, laddie. I rely on my knowledge of human psychology. What did she say when she stung you?"

"I forget. 'Buy a buttercup' or something."

"And then?"

"Then I asked what it was all about, and she said, 'Buttercup Day.'"

"Exactly. And that's all she will need to say to anyone. Is it likely, is it reasonable to suppose, that even in these materialistic days Chivalry has sunk so low that any man will require to be told more, by a girl as pretty as that, than that it is Buttercup Day?" He walked to the window and looked out. "Ah! She's come round into the back garden," he said, with satisfaction. "She seems to be doing a roaring trade. Every second man is wearing a buttercup. She is now putting it across a curate, bless her heart."

"And in a couple of minutes she will probably try

to put it across a plain-clothes detective, and that will be the end."

Ukridge eyed me reproachfully.

"You persist in looking on the gloomy side, Corky. A little more of the congratulatory attitude is what I could wish to see in you, laddie. You do not appear to realize that your old friend's foot is at last on the ladder that leads to wealth. Suppose—putting it at the lowest figure—I net four pounds out of this buttercup business. It goes on Caterpillar in the two o'clock selling race at Kempton. Caterpillar wins, the odds being—let us say—ten to one. Stake and winnings go on Bismuth for the Jubilee Cup, again at ten to one. There you have a nice, clean four hundred pounds of capital, ample for a man of keen business sense to build a fortune on. For, between ourselves, Corky, I have my eye on what looks like the investment of a lifetime."

"Yes?"

"Yes. I was reading about it the other day. A cat ranch out in America."

"A cat ranch?"

"That's it. You collect a hundred thousand cats. Each cat has twelve kittens a year. The skins range from ten cents each for the white ones to seventy-five for the pure black. That gives you twelve million skins per year to sell at an average price of thirty cents per skin, making your annual revenue at a conservative estimate three hundred and sixty thousand dollars. But, you will say, what about overhead expenses?"

"Will I?"

"That has all been allowed for. To feed the cats you start a rat ranch next door. The rats multiply four times as fast as cats, so if you begin with a million rats it gives you four rats per day per cat, which is plenty. You feed the rats on what is left over of the cats after removing the skins, allowing one-fourth of a cat per rat, the business thus becoming automatically self-supporting. The cats will eat the rats, the rats will eat the cats——"

There was a knock upon the door.

"Come in," bellowed Ukridge, irritably. These captains of industry hate to be interrupted when in conference.

It was the butler who had broken in upon his statistics.

"A gentleman to see you, sir," said he.

"Who is he?"

"He did not give his name, sir. He is a gentleman in Holy Orders."

"Not the vicar?" cried Ukridge, in alarm.

"No, sir. The gentleman is a curate. He inquired for Miss Ukridge. I informed him that Miss Ukridge was absent, but that you were on the premises, and he then desired to see you, sir."

"Oh, all right," said Ukridge, resignedly. "Show him in. Though we are running grave risks, Corky," he added, as the door closed. "These curates frequently have subscription lists up their sleeves and are extremely apt, unless you are very firm, to soak you for a donation to the Church Organ Fund or something. Still, let us hope——"

The door opened, and our visitor entered. He was a rather small size in curates, with an engaging, ingenuous face, adorned with a pair of pince-nez. He wore a paper buttercup in his coat; and, directly he began to speak, revealed himself as the possessor of a peculiar stammer.

"Pup-pup-pup——" he said.

"Eh?" said Ukridge.

"Mr. pup-pup-pup Ukridge?"

"Yes. This is my friend, Mr. Corcoran."

I bowed. The curate bowed.

"Take a seat," urged Ukridge, hospitably. "You'll have a drink?"

The visitor raised a deprecatory hand.

"No, thank you," he replied. "I find it more beneficial to my health to abstain entirely from alcoholic liquids. At the University I was a moderate drinker, but since I came down I have found it better to pup-pup-pup completely. But pray do not let me stop you. I am no bigot."

He beamed for an instant in friendly fashion; then there came into his face a look of gravity. Here was a man, one perceived, who had something on his mind.

"I came here, Mr. Ukridge," he said, "on a pup-pup-pup-pup-pup——"

"Parish matter?" I hazarded, to help him out.

He shook his head.

"No, a pup-pup-pup——"

"Pleasure-trip?" suggested Ukridge.

He shook his head again.

"No, a pup-pup-pup uncongenial errand. I understand that Miss Ukridge is absent and that you, as her
nephew, are, therefore, the presiding genius, if I may
use the expression, of these pup-pup-pup festivities."

"Eh?" said Ukridge, fogged.

"I mean that it is to you that complaints should
be made."

"Complaints?"

"Of what is going on in Miss Ukridge's garden—one
might say under her imprimatur."

Ukridge's classical education had been cut short by
the fact that at an early age he had unfortunately been
expelled from the school of which in boyhood's days
we had been fellow-members, and Latin small-talk
was not his forte.   This one passed well over his head.
He looked at me plaintively, and I translated.

"He means," I said, "that your aunt lent her grounds
for this binge and so has a right to early information
about any rough stuff that is being pulled on the
premises."

"Exactly," said the curate.

"But, dash it, laddie," protested Ukridge, now
abreast of the situation, "it's no good complaining of
anything that happens at a charity bazaar.   You
know as well as I do that, when the members of a
Temperance League get together and start selling
things at stalls, anything goes except gouging and
biting.   The only thing to do is to be light on your
feet and keep away."

The curate shook his head sadly.

"I have no complaint to make concerning the

manner in which the stalls are being conducted, Mr.
pup-pup-pup. It is only to be expected that at a
bazaar in aid of a deserving cause the prices of the
various articles on sale will be in excess of those charged
in the ordinary marts of trade. But deliberate and
calculated swindling is another matter."

"Swindling?"

"There is a young woman in the grounds extorting
money from the public on the plea that it is Buttercup
Day. And here is the point, Mr. Ukridge. Butter-
cup Day is the flag-day of the National Orthopaedic
Institute, and is not to take place for some weeks.
This young person is deliberately cheating the public."

Ukridge licked his lips, with a hunted expression.

"Probably a local institution of the same name,"
I suggested.

"That's it," said Ukridge, gratefully. "Just what
I was going to say myself. Probably a local institution. Fresh Air Fund for the poor of the neighbourhood, I shouldn't wonder. I believe I've heard them
talk about it, now I come to think."

The curate refused to consider the theory.

"No," he said. "If that had been so the young
woman would have informed me. In answer to my
questions, her manner was evasive and I could elicit
no satisfactory reply. She merely smiled and repeated
the words 'Buttercup Day.' I feel that the police
should be called in."

"The police!" gurgled Ukridge, pallidly.

"It is our pup-pup duty," said the curate, looking
like a man who writes letters to the Press signed "Pro
Bono Publico."

Ukridge shot out of his chair with a convulsive bound. He grasped my arm and led me to the door.

"Excuse me," he said. "Corky," he whispered tensely, dragging me out into the passage, "go and tell her to leg it—quick!"

"Right!" I said.

"You will no doubt find a constable in the road," roared Ukridge.

"I bet I will," I replied in a clear, carrying voice.

"We can't have this sort of thing going on here," bellowed Ukridge.

"Certainly not," I shouted with enthusiasm.

He returned to the study, and I went forth upon my errand of mercy. I had reached the front door and was about to open it, when it suddenly opened itself, and the next moment I was gazing into the clear blue eyes of Ukridge's Aunt Julia.

"Oh—ah—er!" I said.

There are certain people in this world in whose presence certain other people can never feel completely at their ease. Notable among the people beneath whose gaze I myself experience a sensation of extreme discomfort and guilt is Miss Julia Ukridge, author of so many widely-read novels, and popular after-dinner speaker at the better class of literary reunion. This was the fourth time we had met, and on each of the previous occasions I had felt the same curious illusion of having just committed some particularly unsavoury crime and—what is more—of having done it with swollen hands, enlarged feet, and trousers bagging at the knee on a morning when I had omitted to shave.

I stood and gaped. Although she had no doubt made her entry by the simple process of inserting a latchkey in the front door and turning it, her abrupt appearance had on me the effect of a miracle.

"Mr. Corcoran!" she observed, without pleasure.

"Er——"

"What are you doing here?"

An inhospitable remark; but justified, perhaps, by the circumstances if our previous relations—which had not been of the most agreeable.

"I came to see—er—Stanley."

"Oh?"

"He wanted me with him this afternoon."

"Indeed?" she said; and her manner suggested surprise at what she evidently considered a strange and even morbid taste on her nephew's part.

"We thought—we thought—we both thought you were lecturing up north."

"When I arrived at the club for luncheon I found a telegram postponing my visit," she condescended to explain. "Where is Stanley?"

"In your study."

"I will go there. I wish to see him."

I began to feel like Horatius at the Bridge. It seemed to me that, foe of the human race though Ukridge was in so many respects, it was my duty as a lifelong friend to prevent this woman winning through to him until that curate was well out of the way. I have a great belief in woman's intuition, and I was convinced that, should Miss Julia Ukridge learn that there was a girl in her grounds selling paper buttercups for a non-existent charity, her keen intelligence would leap without the slightest hesitation to the fact of her nephew's complicity in the disgraceful affair. She had had previous experience of Ukridge's financial methods.

In this crisis I thought rapidly.

"Oh, by the way," I said. "It nearly slipped my mind. The—er—the man in charge of all this business told me he particularly wanted to see you directly you came back."

"What do you mean by the man in charge of all this business?"

"The fellow who got up the bazaar, you know."

"Do you mean Mr. Sims, the president of the Temperance League?"

"That's right. He told me he wanted to see you."

"How could he possibly know that I should be coming back?"

"Oh, in case you did, I mean." I had what Ukridge would have called an inspiration from above. "I think he wants you to say a few words."

I doubt if anything else would have shifted her. There came into her eyes, softening their steely glitter for a moment, that strange light which is seen only in the eyes of confirmed public speakers who are asked to say a few words.

"Well, I will go and see him."

She turned away, and I bounded back to the study. The advent of the mistress of the house had materially altered my plans for the afternoon. What I proposed to do now was to inform Ukridge of her arrival, advise him to eject the curate with all possible speed, give

him my blessing, and then slide quietly and unosten-
tatiously away, without any further formalities of
farewell. I am not unduly sensitive, but there had
been that in Miss Ukridge's manner at our recent
meeting which told me that I was not her ideal guest.

I entered the study. The curate was gone, and
Ukridge, breathing heavily, was fast asleep in an
arm-chair.

The disappearance of the curate puzzled me for a
moment. He was rather an insignificant little man,
but not so insignificant that I would not have noticed
him if he had passed me while I was standing at the
front door. And then I saw that the French windows
were open.

It seemed to me that there was nothing to keep me.
The strong distaste for this house which I had never
lost since my first entry into it had been growing, and
now the great open spaces called to me with an imperious voice. I turned softly, and found my hostess
standing in the doorway.

"Oh, ah!" I said; and once more was afflicted by
that curious sensation of having swelled in a very
loathsome manner about the hands and feet. I have
observed my hands from time to time during my life
and have never been struck by anything particularly
hideous about them: but whenever I encounter Miss
Julia Ukridge they invariably take on the appearance
and proportions of uncooked hams.

"Did you tell me, Mr. Corcoran," said the woman in
that quiet, purring voice which must lose her so many
friends, not only in Wimbledon but in the larger world

outside, "that you saw Mr. Sims and he said that he wished to speak to me?"

"That's right."

"Curious," said Miss Ukridge. "I find that Mr. Sims is confined to his bed with a chill and has not been here to-day."

I could sympathize with Mr. Sim's chills. I felt as if I had caught one myself. I would—possibly—have made some reply, but at this moment an enormous snore proceeded from the arm-chair behind me, and such was my overwrought condition that I leaped like a young ram.

"Stanley!" cried Miss Ukridge, sighting the chair.

Another snore rumbled through the air, competing with the music of the merry-go-round. Miss Ukridge advanced and shook her nephew's arm.

"I think," I said, being in the frame of mind when one does say silly things of that sort, "I think he's asleep."

"Asleep!" said Miss Ukridge briefly. Her eye fell on the half-empty glass on the table, and she shuddered austerely.

The interpretation which she obviously placed on the matter seemed incredible to me. On the stage and in motion-pictures one frequently sees victims of drink keel over in a state of complete unconsciousness after a single glass, but Ukridge was surely of sterner stuff.

"I can't understand it," I said.

"Indeed!" said Miss Ukridge.

"Why, I have only been out of the room half a minute, and when I left him he was talking to a curate."

"A curate?"

"Absolutely a curate. It's hardly likely, is it, that when he was talking to a curate he would——"

My speech for the defence was cut short by a sudden, sharp noise which, proceeding from immediately behind me, caused me once more to quiver convulsively.

"Well, sir?" said Miss Ukridge.

She was looking past me; and, turning, I perceived that a stranger had joined us. He was standing in the French windows, and the noise which had startled me had apparently been caused by him rapping on the glass with the knob of a stick."

"Miss Ukridge?" said the newcomer.

He was one of those hard-faced, keen-eyed men. There clung about him, as he advanced into the room, a subtle air of authority. That he was a man of character and resolution was proved by the fact that he met Miss Ukridge's eye without a tremor.

"I am Miss Ukridge. Might I inquire——"

The visitor looked harder-faced and more keen-eyed than ever.

"My name is Dawson. From the Yard."

"What yard?" asked the lady of the house, who, it seemed, did not read detective stories.

"Scotland Yard!"

"Oh!"

"I have come to warn you, Miss Ukridge," said Mr. Dawson, looking at me as if I were a blood-stain, "to be on your guard. One of the greatest rascals in the profession is hanging about your grounds."

"Then why don't you arrest him?" demanded Miss Ukridge. The visitor smiled faintly.

"Because I want to get him good," he said.

"Get him good? Do you mean reform him?"

"I do not mean reform him," said Mr. Dawson, grimly. "I mean that I want to catch him trying on something worth pulling him in for. There's no sense in taking a man like Stuttering Sam for being a suspected person."

"Stuttering Sam!" I cried, and Mr. Dawson eyed me keenly once more, this time almost as intently as if I had been the blunt instrument with which the murder was committed.

"Eh?" he said.

"Oh, nothing. Only it's curious——"

"What's curious?"

"Oh, no, it couldn't be. This fellow was a curate. A most respectable man."

"Have you seen a curate who stuttered?" exclaimed Mr. Dawson.

"Why, yes. He——"

"Hullo!" said Mr. Dawson. "Who's this?"

"That," replied Miss Ukridge, eyeing the arm-chair with loathing, "is my nephew Stanley."

"Sound sleeper."

"I prefer not to talk about him."

"Tell me about this curate," said Mr. Dawson, brusquely.

"Well, he came in——"

"Came in? In here?"

"Yes."

"Why?"

"Well——"

"He must have had some story. What was it?"

I thought it judicious, in the interests of my sleeping friend, to depart somewhat from the precise truth.

"He—er—I think he said something about being interested in Miss Ukridge's collection of snuff-boxes."

"Have you a collection of snuff-boxes, Miss Ukridge?"

"Yes."

"Where do you keep them?"

"In the drawing-room."

"Take me there, if you please."

"But I don't understand."

Mr. Dawson clicked his tongue in an annoyed manner. He seemed to be an irritable sleuth-hound.

"I should have thought the thing was clear enough by this time. This man worms his way into your house with a plausible story, gets rid of this gentleman here—— How did he get rid of you?"

"Oh, I just went, you know. I thought I would like a stroll."

"Oh? Well, having contrived to be alone with your nephew, Miss Ukridge, he slips knock-out drops in his drink——"

"Knock-out drops?"

"A drug of some kind," explained Mr. Dawson, chafing at her slowness of intelligence.

"But the man was a curate!"

Mr. Dawson barked shortly.

"Posing as a curate is the thing Stuttering Sam

does best. He works the races in that character. Is this the drawing-room?"

It was. And it did not need the sharp, agonized cry which proceeded from its owner's lips to tell us that the worst had happened. The floor was covered with splintered wood and broken glass.

"They've gone!" cried Miss Ukridge.

It is curious how differently the same phenomenon can strike different people. Miss Ukridge was a frozen statue of grief. Mr. Dawson, on the other hand, seemed pleased. He stroked his short moustache with an air of indulgent complacency, and spoke of neat jobs. He described Stuttering Sam as a Tough Baby, and gave it as his opinion that the absent one might justly be considered one of the lads and not the worst of them.

"What shall I do?" wailed Miss Ukridge. I was sorry for the woman. I did not like her, but she was suffering.

"The first thing to do," said Mr. Dawson, briskly, "is to find how much the fellow has got away with. Have you any other valuables in the house?"

"My jewels are in my bedroom."

"Where?"

"I keep them in a box in the dress-cupboard."

"Well, it's hardly likely that he would find them there, but I'd better go and see. You be taking a look round in here and make a complete list of what has been stolen."

"All my snuff-boxes are gone."

"Well, see if there is anything else missing. Where is your bedroom?"

"On the first floor, facing the front."

"Right."

Mr. Dawson, all briskness and efficiency, left us. I was sorry to see him go. I had an idea that it would not be pleasant being left alone with this bereaved woman. Nor was it.

"Why on earth," said Miss Ukridge, rounding on me as if I had been a relation, "did you not suspect this man when he came in?"

"Why, I—he——"

"A child ought to have been able to tell that he was not a real curate."

"He seemed——' "

"Seemed!" She wandered restlessly about the room, and suddenly a sharp cry proceeded from her. "My jade Buddha!"

"I beg your pardon?"

"That scoundrel has stolen my jade Buddha. Go and tell the detective."

"Certainly."

"Go on! What are you waiting for?"

I fumbled at the handle.

"I don't seem able to get the door open," I explained, meekly.

"Tchah!" said Miss Ukridge, swooping down. One of the rooted convictions of each member of the human race is that he or she is able without difficulty to open a door which has baffled their fellows. She took the handle and gave it a vigorous tug. The door creaked but remained unresponsive.

"What's the matter with the thing?" exclaimed Miss Ukridge, petulantly.

"It's stuck."

"I know it has stuck.   Please do something at once.
Good gracious, Mr. Corcoran, surely you are at least
able to open a drawing-room door?"

It seemed, put in that tone of voice, a feat sufficiently
modest for a man of good physique and fair general
education; but I was reluctantly compelled to confess,
after a few more experiments, that it was beyond my
powers.   This appeared to confirm my hostess in the
opinion, long held by her, that I was about the most
miserable worm that an inscrutable Providence had
ever permitted to enter the world.

She did not actually say as much, but she sniffed,
and I interpreted her meaning exactly.

"Ring the bell!"

I rang the bell.

"Ring it again!"

I rang it again.

"Shout!"

I shouted.

"Go on shouting!"

I went on shouting.   I was in good voice that day.
I shouted "Hi!"; I shouted "Here!"; I shouted
"Help!"; I also shouted in a broad, general way.   It
was a performance which should have received more
than a word of grateful thanks.   But all Miss Ukridge
said, when I paused for breath, was:

"Don't whisper!"

I nursed my aching vocal cords in a wounded silence.

"Help!" cried Miss Ukridge.

Considered as a shout, it was not in the same class as

mine.   It lacked body, vim, and even timbre.   But,
by that curious irony which governs human affairs, it
produced results.   Outside the door a thick voice spoke
in answer.

"What's up?"

"Open this door!"

The handle rattled.

"It's stuck," said a voice, which I now recognized
as that of my old friend, Stanley Featherstonehaugh
Ukridge.

"I know it has stuck.   Is that you, Stanley?   See
what is causing it to stick."

A moment of silence followed.   Investigations were
apparently in progress without.

"There's a wedge jammed under it."

"Well, take it out at once."

"I'll have to get a knife or something."

Another interval for rest and meditation succeeded.
Miss Ukridge paced the floor with knit brows; while I
sidled into a corner and stood there feeling a little like
an inexperienced young animal-trainer who has
managed to get himself locked into the lions' den and
is trying to remember what Lesson Three of his corre-
spondence course said he ought to do in such circumstances.

Footsteps sounded outside, and then a wrenching
and scratching.   The door opened and we beheld on
the mat Ukridge, with a carving-knife in his hand,
looking headachy and dishevelled, and the butler, his
professional poise rudely disturbed and his face stained
with coal-dust.

It was characteristic of Miss Ukridge that it was to the erring domestic rather than the rescuing nephew that she turned first.

"Barter," she hissed, as far as a woman, even of her intellectual gifts, is capable of hissing the word "Barter," "why didn't you come when I rang?"

"I did not hear the bell, madam. I was——"

"You must have heard the bell."

"No, madam."

"Why not?"

"Because I was in the coal-cellar, madam."

"What on earth were you doing in the coal-cellar?"

"I was induced to go there, madam, by a man. He intimidated me with a pistol. He then locked me in."

"What! What man?"

"A person with a short moustache and penetrating eyes. He——"

A raconteur with a story as interesting as his to tell might reasonably have expected to be allowed to finish it, but butler Barter at this point ceased to grip his audience. With a gasping moan his employer leaped past him, and we heard her running up the stairs.

Ukridge turned to me plaintively.

"What is all this, laddie? Gosh, I've got a headache. What has been happening?"

"The curate put knock-out drops in your drink, and then——"

I have seldom seen anyone display such poignant emotion as Ukridge did at that moment.

"The curate! It's a little hard. Upon my Sam,

it's a trifle thick.   Corky, old horse, I have travelled
all over the world in tramp-steamers and what not.
I have drunk in waterfront saloons from Montevideo
to Cardiff.   And the only time anyone has ever
succeeded in doctoring the stuff on me it was done in
Wimbledon—and by a curate.   Tell me, laddie, are
all curates like that?   Because, if so——"

"He has also pinched your aunt's collection of
snuff-boxes."

"The curate?"

"Yes."

"Golly!" said Ukridge in a low, reverent voice, and
I could see a new respect for the Cloth dawning within
him.

"And then this other fellow came along—his accom-
plice, pretending to be a detective—and locked us in
and shut the butler in the coal-cellar.   And I rather
fancy he has got away with your aunt's jewels."

A piercing scream from above rent the air.

"He has," I said briefly.   "Well, old man, I think
I'll be going."

"Corky," said Ukridge, "stand by me!"

I shook my head.

"In any reasonable circumstances, yes.   But I
will not meet your aunt again just now.   In a year or
so, perhaps, but not now."

Hurrying footsteps sounded on the staircase.

"Good-bye," I said, pushing past and heading for
the open.   "I must be off.   Thanks for a very pleasant
afternoon."

Money was tight in those days, but it seemed to me

next morning that an outlay of twopence on a telephone call to Heath House could not be considered an
unjustifiable extravagance. I was conscious of a
certain curiosity to learn at long range what had
happened after I had removed myself on the previous
afternoon.

"Are you there?" said a grave voice in answer to
my ring.

"Is that Barter?"

"Yes, sir."

"This is Mr. Corcoran. I want to speak to Mr.
Ukridge."

"Mr. Ukridge is no longer here, sir.   He left perhaps
an hour ago."

"Oh? Do you mean left—er—for ever?"

"Yes, sir."

"Oh! Thanks."

I rang off and, pondering deeply, returned to my
rooms. I was not surprised to be informed by Bowles,
my landlord, that Ukridge was in my sitting-room.
It was this storm-tossed man's practice in times of
stress to seek refuge with me.

"Hullo, laddie," said Ukridge in a graveyard
voice.

"So here you are."

"Here I am."

"She kicked you out?"

Ukridge winced slightly, as at some painful recol-
lection.

"Words passed, old horse, and in the end we decided
that we were better apart."

"I don't see why she should blame you for what happened."

"A woman like my aunt, Corky, is capable of blaming anybody for anything. And so I start life again, laddie, a penniless man, with no weapons against the great world but my vision and my brain."

I endeavoured to attract his attention to the silver lining.

"You're all right," I said. "You're just where you wanted to be. You have the money which your buttercup girl collected."

A strong spasm shook my poor friend, causing, as always happened with him in moments of mental agony, his collar to shoot off its stud and his glasses to fall from his nose.

"The money that girl collected," he replied, "is not available. It has passed away. I saw her this morning and she told me."

"Told you what?"

"That a curate came up to her in the garden while she was selling those buttercups and—in spite of a strong stammer—put it to her so eloquently that she was obtaining money under false pretences that she gave him the entire takings for his Church Expenses Fund and went home, resolved to lead a better life. Women are an unstable, emotional sex, laddie. Have as little to do with them as possible. And, for the moment, give me a drink, old horse, and mix it fairly strong. These are the times that try men's souls."

UKRIDGE AND THE OLD STEPPER

UKRIDGE AND THE OLD STEPPER

"CORKY, old horse," said Stanley Featherstone-haugh Ukridge, in a stunned voice, "this is the most amazing thing I have heard in the whole course of my existence. I'm astounded. You could knock me down with a feather."

"I wish I had one."

"This suit?—this shabby, worn-out suit?—you don't really mean to stand there and tell me that you actually *wanted* this ragged, seedy, battered old suit? Why, upon my honest Sam, when I came on it while rummaging through your belongings yesterday, I thought it was just something you had discarded years ago and forgotten to give to the deserving poor."

I spoke my mind. Any unbiased judge would have admitted that I had cause for warmth. Spring, coming to London in a burst of golden sunshine, was calling imperiously to all young men to rejoice in their youth, to put on their new herringbone-pattern lounge suits and go out and give the populace an eyeful; and this I had been prevented from doing by the fact that my new suit had mysteriously disappeared.

After a separation of twenty-four hours, I had just met it in Piccadilly with Ukridge inside it.

I continued to speak, and was beginning to achieve a certain eloquence, when from a taxi-cab beside us there alighted a small, dapper old gentleman, who might have been a duke or one of the better-class ambassadors or something of that sort. He wore a pointed white beard, a silk hat, lavender spats, an Ascot tie, and a gardenia; and if anyone had told me that such a man could have even a nodding acquaintance with S. F. Ukridge, I should have laughed hollowly. Furthermore, if I had been informed that Ukridge, warmly greeted by such a man, would have ignored him and passed coldly on, I should have declined to believe it.

Nevertheless, both these miracles happened.

"Stanley!" cried the old gentleman. "Bless my soul, I haven't seen you for years." And he spoke, what is more, as if he regretted the fact, not as if he had had a bit of luck that made my mouth water. "Come and have some lunch, my dear boy."

"Corky," said Ukridge, eyeing him stonily for a moment and speaking in a low, strained voice, "let us be getting along."

"But did you hear him?" I gasped, as he hurried me away. "He asked you to lunch."

"I heard him. Corky, old boy," said Ukridge, gravely, "I'll tell you. That bloke is best avoided."

"Who is he?"

"An uncle of mine."

"But he seemed respectable."

"That is to say, a step-uncle. Or would you call him step-step? He married my late step-mother's

step-sister. I'm not half sure," said Ukridge, pondering, "that step-step-step wouldn't be the correct
description."

These were deep waters, into which I was not
prepared to plunge.

"But what did you want to cut him for?"

"It's a long story. I'll tell you at lunch."

I raised a passionate hand.

"If you think that after pinching my spring
suiting you're going to get so much as a crust of
bread——"

"Calm yourself, laddie. You're lunching with me.
Largely on the strength of this suit, I managed to get
past the outer defences of the Foreign Office just now
and touch old George Tupper for a fiver. Joy will be
unconfined."

"Corky," said Ukridge, thoughtfully, spreading
caviare on a piece of toast in the Regent grill-room
some ten minutes later, "do you ever brood on what
might have been?"

"I'm doing it now. I might have been wearing
that suit."

"There is no need to go into that again," said
Ukridge, with dignity. "I have explained that little
misunderstanding—explained it fully. What I mean
is, do you ever brood on the inscrutable workings of
Fate and reflect how, but for this or that, you might
have been—well, that or this? For instance, but for
the old Stepper I would by now be the mainstay of a
vast business, and in all probability happily married

to a charming girl and the father of half a dozen prattling children."

"In which case, if there is anything in heredity, I should have had to keep my spring suits in a Safe Deposit."

"Corky, old horse," said Ukridge, pained, "you keep harping on this beastly suit of yours. It shows an ungracious spirit which I do not like to see. What was I saying?"

"You were babbling about Fate."

"Ah, yes."

Fate (said Ukridge) is odd. Rummy. You can't say it isn't. Lots of people have noticed it. And one of the rummiest things about it is the way it seems to take a delight in patting you on the head and lulling you into security and then suddenly steering your foot on to the banana-skin. Just when things appear to be going smoothest, bang comes the spanner into the machinery and there you are.

Take this business I'm going to tell you about. Just before it happened, I had begun to look upon myself as Fortune's favourite child. Everything was breaking right in the most astounding fashion. My Aunt Julia, having sailed for America on one of her lecturing tours, had lent me her cottage at Market Deeping in Sussex till her return, with instructions to the local tradesmen to let me have the necessaries of life and chalk them up to her. From some source which at the moment I cannot recollect, I had snaffled two pairs of white flannel trousers and a tennis racket.

And finally, after a rather painful scene in the course of which I was compelled to allude to him as a pig-headed bureaucrat, I had contrived to get a couple of quid out of old Tuppy. My position was solid. I ought to have known that luck like that couldn't last.

Now, in a parting conversation on the platform at Waterloo while waiting for the boat-train to start, Aunt Julia had revealed the fact that her motive in sticking me down at her cottage had not been simply to ensure that I had a pleasant summer. It seemed that at Deeping Hall, the big house of the locality, there resided a certain Sir Edward Bayliss, O.B.E., a bird deeply immersed in the jute industry. To this day I have never quite got it clear what jute really is, but, anyway, this Sir Edward was a man to keep in with, for his business had ramifications everywhere and endless openings for the bright young beginner. He was, moreover, a great admirer of my aunt's novels, and she told me in a few and, in parts, tactless words that what I was going down there for was to ingratiate myself with him and land a job. Which, she said—and this was where I thought her remarks lacked taste—would give me a chance of doing something useful and ceasing to be what she called a wastrel and an idler.

Idler! I'll trouble you! As if for a single day in my life, Corky, I had ever not buzzed about doing the work of ten men. Why, take the mere getting of that couple of quid from old Tuppy, for instance. Simple as it sounds, I doubt if Napoleon could have done it.

Tuppy, sterling fellow though he is, has his bad morn-
ings. He comes down to the office and finds a sharp
note from the President of Uruguay or someone on his
desk, and it curdles the milk of human kindness within
him. On these occasions he becomes so tight that he
could carry an armful of eels up five flights of stairs
and not drop one. And yet in less than a quarter of
an hour I had got a couple of quid out of him.

Oh, well, women say these things.

Well, I packed a suit-case and took the next train
down to Market Deeping. And the first thing for you
to do, Corky, before I go on, is to visualize the general
lay-out of the place. My aunt's cottage (Journey's
End) was here, where this bit of bread is. Here, next
to it, where I've put the potato, was a smallish house
(Pondicherry) belonging to Colonel Bayliss, the jute-
fancier's brother. The gardens adjoined, but anything
in the way of neighbourly fraternizing was prevented
for the moment by the fact that the Colonel was away—
at Harrogate, I learned later, trying to teach his liver
to take a joke. All this expanse here—I'll mark it
with a splash of Worcester Sauce—was the park of
Deeping Hall, beyond which was the Hall itself and all
the gardens, messuages, pleasaunces, and so forth that
you'd expect.

Got it now? Right.

Well, as you can see from the diagram, the park of
the Hall abutted—if that's the word I want—on the
back garden of my cottage; and judge of my emotions
when, as I smoked an after-breakfast pipe under the
trees on the first morning after my arrival, I saw the

most extraordinarily pretty girl riding there.   Hither
and thither.   She came so close once that I could have
hit her with an apple.   Not that I did, of course.

I don't know if you have ever been in love at first
sight, Corky?   One moment I was looking idly through
the hedge to see where the hoof-beats came from; the
next I was electrified from head to foot, and in the
bushes around me a million birds had begun to toot.
I gathered at once that this must be the O.B.E.'s
daughter, or something on those lines, and I found my
whole attitude towards the jute business, which up
till now had been what you might call lukewarm,
changing in a flash.   It didn't take me more than a
second to realize that a job involving a connection
with this girl was practically the ideal one.

I called at the Hall that afternoon, mentioned my
name, and from the very start everything went like
a breeze.

I don't want to boast, Corky—and, of course, I'm
speaking now of some years ago, before Life had
furrowed my brow and given my eyes that haunted
look—but I may tell you frankly that at the time when
these things happened I was a rather dazzling spectacle.
I had just had my hair cut and the flannel bags fitted
me to a nicety, and altogether I was an asset—yes, old
horse, a positive asset to any social circle.   The days
flew by.   The O.B.E. was chummy.   The girl—her
name was Myrtle, and I think she had found life at
Market Deeping a bit on the slow side till I arrived—
always seemed glad to see me.   I was the petted
young neighbour.

And then one afternoon in walked the Stepper.

There have been occasions in my life, Corky, when, if I had seen a strange man walking up the path to the front door of the house where I was living, I should have ducked through the back premises and remained concealed in the raspberry bushes till he had blown over. But it so happened that at this time my financial affairs were on a sound and solid basis and I hadn't a single creditor in the world. So I went down and opened the door and found him beaming on the mat.

"Stanley Ukridge?" he said.

"Yes," I said.

"I called at your aunt's house at Wimbledon the other day and they told me you were here. I'm your Uncle Percy from Australia, my boy. I married your late step-mother's step-sister Alice."

I don't suppose anybody with a pointed white beard has ever received a heartier welcome. I don't know if you have any pet day-dream, Corky, but mine had always been the sudden appearance of the rich uncle from Australia you read so much about in novels. The old-fashioned novels, I mean, the ones where the hero isn't a dope-fiend. And here he was, looking as I had always expected him to look. You saw his spats just now, you observed his gardenia. Well, on the afternoon of which I'm speaking, he was just as spatted, fully as gardenia-ed, and in addition wore in his tie something that looked like a miniature Koh-i-noor.

"Well, well, well!" I said.

"Well, well, well!" he said.

He patted my back. I patted his. He said he was a lonely old man who had come back to England to spend his declining years with some congenial relative. I said I was just as keen on finding uncles as he was on spotting nephews. The thing was a love-feast.

"You can put me up for a week or two, Stanley?"

"Delighted."

"Nice little place you have here."

"Glad you like it."

"Wants a bit of smartening up, though," said the Stepper, looking round at the appointments and not seeming to think a lot of them. Aunt Julia had furnished the cottage fairly sparsely.

"Perhaps you're right."

"Some comfortable chairs, eh?"

"Fine."

"And a sofa."

"Splendid."

"And perhaps a nice little summer-house for the garden. Have you a summer-house?"

I said: "No, no summer-house."

"I'll be looking about for one," said the Stepper.

And everything I had read about rich uncles from Australia seemed to me to have come true. Spacious is the only word to describe his attitude. He was like some Eastern monarch giving the Court architect specifications for a new palace. This, I told myself, was how these fine, breezy, Empire-building fellows always were—generous, open-handed, gaily reckless of expense. I wished I had met him earlier.

"And now, my boy," said the old Stepper, sticking out from six to eight inches of tongue and running same round his lips, "where do you keep the drinks?"

I've always maintained, and I always will maintain, that there's nothing in this world to beat a real bachelor establishment. Men have a knack of making themselves comfortable which few women can ever achieve. My Aunt Julia's idea of a chair, for instance, was something antique made to the order of the Spanish Inquisition. The Stepper had the right conception. Men arrived in vans and unloaded things with slanting backs and cushioned seats, and whenever I wasn't over at the Hall I wallowed in these.

The Stepper wallowed in them all the time. Occasionally he put in an hour or so in the summer-house—for he had caused a summer-house to appear at the bottom of the garden—but mostly you would find him indoors with all the windows shut and something to drink at his elbow. He said he had had so much fresh air in Australia that what he wanted now was something he could scoop out with a spoon.

Once or twice I tried to get him over to the Hall, but he would have none of it. He said from what he knew of O.B.E.'s he wouldn't be allowed to take his boots off, and ran, moreover, a grave risk of being offered barley-water. Apparently he had once met a teetotal O.B.E. in Sydney and was prejudiced. However, he was most sympathetic when I told him about Myrtle. He said that, though he wasn't any too keen on matrimony as an institution, he was broad-minded enough to realize that there might quite possibly be women in the world unlike his late wife. Concerning whom, he added that the rabbit was not, as had been generally stated, Australia's worst pest.

"Tell me of this girl, my boy," he said. "You squeeze her a good deal in dark corners, no doubt?"

"Certainly not," I said, stiffly.

"Then things have changed very much since my young days. What do you do?"

I said I looked at her quite a lot and hung on her every word and all that sort of thing.

"Do you give her presents?"

He had touched on a subject which I had intended to bring up myself when I could find an opening. You see, Myrtle's birthday was approaching; and, though nothing had actually been said about any little gift, I had sensed a certain expectation in the air. Even the best of girls are like that, Corky. They say how old they feel with another birthday coming along so soon, and then they look brightly at you.

"Well, as a matter of fact, Uncle Percy," I said, flicking a speck of dust off his sleeve, "I was rather planning something of the kind, if only I could see my way to managing it. It's her birthday next week, Uncle Percy, and it crossed my mind that if I could stumble on somebody who could slip me a few quid, something might possibly be done about it, Uncle Percy."

He waved his hand in an Australian sort of way.

"Leave it all to me, my boy."

"Oh, no, really!"

"I insist."

"Oh, if you insist."

"My late wife was your late step-mother's step-sister, and blood is thicker than water. Now, let me see," mused the old Stepper, wriggling his feet a couple of inches farther on to the table and knitting the brow a bit. "What shall it be? Jewellery? No. Girls like their little bit of jewellery, but perhaps it would scarcely do. I have it. A sundial."

"A what?" I said.

"A sundial," said the old Stepper. "What could be a more pretty and tasteful gift? No doubt she has a little garden of her own, some sequestered nook which she tends with her own hands and where she wanders in maiden meditation on summer evenings. If so, she needs a sundial."

"But, Uncle Percy," I said doubtfully, "do you really think——? My idea was rather that if you could possibly let me have a fiver—or say a tenner—to make up the round sum——"

"She draws a sundial," said the old Stepper, firmly, "and likes it."

I tried to reason with the man.

"But you can't get a sundial," I urged.

"I can get a sundial," said the old Stepper, waving his whisky and soda with a good deal of asperity. "I can get anything. Sundials, summer-houses, elephants if you want them. I'm noted for it. Show me the man who says that Charles Percy Cuthbertson can't get a sundial, and I'll give him the lie in his teeth. That's where I'll give it him. In his teeth!"

And, as he seemed to be warming up a bit, we left it at that. I never dreamed that he would make good, of course. You'll admit, I think, Corky, that I'm a pretty gifted fellow, but if anyone called upon me at practically a moment's notice to produce a sundial, I should be nonplussed. Nevertheless, bright and early on the morning of Myrtle's birthday I heard a yodel under my window, and there he was, standing beside a wheelbarrow containing sundial complete as per invoice. It all seemed to me more like magic than anything, and I began to feel like Aladdin. Apparently my job from now on was simply to rub the lamp and the Stepper would do the rest.

"There you are, my boy," he said, dusting the thing off with a handkerchief and regarding it in a fatherly sort of way. "You give the little lady that and she'll let you cuddle her behind the front door."

This struck a slightly jarring note, of course. He seemed to me to be taking an entirely too earthy view of my great love, which was intensely spiritual. But it was not the moment to say so.

"That'll make her clap her hands prettily. That'll send her singing about the house."

"She ought to like it," I agreed.

"Of course she'll like it. She'd damn' well better like it. Show me a wholesome, sweet-minded English girl who doesn't like a sundial and I'll paste her on the nose," said the Stepper, warmly. "Why, it's got a motto and everything."

And so it had. We hadn't spotted it at first, the contrivance having been more or less covered with moss; but the Stepper had worked briskly with a table-knife and now you got a good view of it. Some rot, if I recollect rightly, about ye sunne and ye shoures, carved in old English letters. It seemed to alter the whole aspect of the sundial—lift it, as it were, into a higher and more dignified class; and for the first time I began to get really enthusiastic.

"This is the goods, Uncle Percy," I said. "This is the right stuff. How can I thank you enough?"

"You can't," said the Stepper.

"I'll tell you what the procedure here is," I said. "I'll take this thing over to the Hall this morning and ask Myrtle and her father to come to tea. They can't refuse when they've just been handed a sundial like this."

"Certainly," said the Stepper. "A very good idea. Ask them here to tea, and I'll make the house a bower of roses."

"Can you get roses?"

"Can I get roses! Don't keep asking me if I can get things. Of course I can get roses. And eggs, too."

"We shan't want eggs."

"We shall want eggs," said the Stepper, beginning to hot up again. "If eggs are good enough for me, they're good enough for the pop-eyed daughter of a blighted O.B.E. Or don't you think so?"

"Oh, quite, Uncle Percy, quite," I said.

I would have liked to inform him that Myrtle wasn't pop-eyed, but he didn't seem in the mood.

Any doubts I may have had as to the acceptability

of my birthday present vanished as soon as, with
infinite sweat, I had wheeled it across the park in its
barrow. The Stepper had had the right idea. Myrtle
was all over the sundial. I sprang the tea invitation,
and for the moment it looked as if there was going to
be a hitch. Her Uncle Philip, the Colonel, it seemed,
was due to materialize that afternoon. He always
made a point of being present for his niece's birthday,
however far he had to come to be there, and he would
be terribly hurt if he arrived and found she had let
him down. What to do?

"Bring him along," I said, of course. And we
arranged it on those lines. The Colonel, on getting
off the train and going to the Hall, would find a note
instructing him to hoof it across the park and come and
revel at Journey's End. I didn't say so to Myrtle,
for the time did not seem to me ripe, but what it
amounted to, I felt, was that the Colonel would come
seeking a niece and would find in addition a nephew.
Than which, for a bloke getting on in years and needing
all the loved ones round him that could be assembled,
what could be a jollier surprise? I disagree with you,
Corky. It does not depend on the kind of nephew.
Any nephew is a boon to a lonely bachelor like that.

So I wheeled the wheelbarrow back to the cottage,
feeling that all was well. And at about half-past four
the maid who came in from the village by the day to
do our cooking and washing-up announced Sir Edward
and Miss Bayliss.

I'm an old campaigner now, Corky, and Fate has to
take its coat off and spit on its hands a bit if it wants

to fool me. To-day, when Fate offers me something apparently gilt-edged, I look it over coldly and assume, till it has been proved otherwise, that attached to it somewhere there is a string. But at the time of which I am speaking I was younger, more buoyant, more credulous; and I honestly supposed that this tea-party of mine was going to be the success it seemed at the start.

The thing had got under way without a suspicion of anything in the nature of a disaster. In the first place, the maid had responded to my coaching in the most admirable manner. A simple child of the soil, her natural disposition would have been to bung the door open and bellow: "They're here!" Instead of which, she had done the announcing with a style and polish that gave the whole proceedings a tone from the very outset. Secondly, Sir Edward had not bumped his head against the beam on the ceiling just inside the front door. And, lastly, though the Stepper's roses were present in wonderful profusion, he himself hadn't shown up. And that seemed to me the biggest stroke of luck of the lot.

You see, the old Stepper wasn't everybody's money. To begin with, he had an apparently incurable dislike of O.B.E.'s, and then he combined with a hot-blooded and imperious nature the odd belief that eggs were a suitable food for adult human beings at five o'clock in the afternoon. And he was so touchy, too, so ready to resent opposition. I had had visions of him standing over Sir Edward and shoving eggs down his throat at the point of a table-knife. He was better away, and I hoped he had fallen into a ditch and couldn't get out.

From the moment the first drop of tea was poured everything went as smooth as oil. In recent years, Corky, affairs have so shaped themselves that you have had the opportunity of seeing me mainly in the capacity of a guest; but you can take it from me that, vouchsafed the right conditions, I can be a very sparkling host.   Give me a roof over my head, plenty of buttered toast, and no creditors in sight, and I shine with the best of them.

On the present occasion I was at the top of my form. I handed cups. I slid the toast about. I prattled merrily. And I could see the old boy was impressed. These O.B.E.'s are silent, reserved men, and for a while he just looked at me from time to time in a meditative way.   Then, as he was dipping into his third cup of tea, out he came into the open and began to talk turkey.

"Your aunt . . . Have you heard from her, by the way?"

"Not yet.   I suppose she's very busy."

"I imagine so.   An energetic woman."

"Very.   All we Ukridges are energetic.   We do not spare ourselves."

"Your aunt," resumed the old boy, swallowing some more tea, "gave me the impression in one of the conversations we had before she left England that you were looking out for an opening in the world of commerce."

"Yes," I said.   I stroked my chin thoughtfully and tried to look as much as possible like Charles M. Schwab being approached by the President of the United States Steel Corporation with a view to a merger. You've got to show these birds that you've a proper sense of your own value. Start right with them, or it's no use starting at all. "I might accept commercial employment if the salary and prospects were undeniable."

He cleared his throat.

"In my own business," he was beginning, "the jute business——"

Just then the door opened and the maid appeared. She was one of those snorting girls, and she snorted something about a gentleman. I couldn't get it.

"Who's a gentleman?" I said.

"Outside. He says he wants to see you."

"It must be Uncle Philip," said Myrtle.

"Of course," I said. "Show him in. Don't keep him waiting, my good girl. Show him in at once."

And a moment later in came a bloke. Obviously not the Colonel, for Myrtle and the O.B.E. gave no sign of recognition. Then who? The man was a perfect stranger to me.

However, I played the host.

"Good afternoon," I said, affably.

"Afternoon," said the bloke.

"Take a chair," I said.

"I'm going to take all the chairs," he said. "And the sofa, too. I'm from the Mammoth Furnishing Company, and the cheque for the deposit on this stuff has been returned Refer to Drawer."

It is not too much to say, Corky, that I reeled. Yes,

laddie, your old friend tottered and would have fallen
had he not clutched at a chair.   And, from the look in
the bloke's eye, it began to seem that my chances of
clutching at that particular chair were likely to be
very soon a thing of the past.   He had one of those
brooding eyes.   Two, probably, only there was a
patch over the left one.   I think someone must have
hit him there.   A fellow like that could scarcely go
through life without getting punched in the eye.

"But, my dear old horse——" I began.

"It's no use arguing.   We've written twice and
never got an answer, and I've instructions from the
firm to take the stuff."

"But we're using it."

"Not now," said the blighter.   "You've finished."

I look back on that moment, Corky, old boy, as one
of the worst in my career.   It is always a nervous
business for a fellow to entertain for the first time the
girl he loves and her father; and, believe me, it doesn't
help pass things off when a couple of the proletariat in
shirt-sleeves surge into the room and start carrying out
all the chairs.   Conversation during the proceedings
was, you might say, at a standstill; and even after the
operations were over it wasn't any too easy to get it
going again.

"Some absurd mistake," I said.

"No doubt," said the O.B.E.

"I shall write those people a very stiff letter to-
night."

"No doubt."

"That furniture was bought by my uncle, one of the

wealthiest men in Australia. It's absurd to suppose
that a man of his standing would——"

"No doubt. Myrtle, my dear, I think we will be
going."

Then, Corky, I spread myself. On not a few
occasions in a life that has had its ups and downs I have
been compelled to do some impressive talking, but
now I surpassed all previous efforts. The thought of
all that was slipping away from me spurred me to
heights I have never reached before or since. And
gradually, little by little, I made headway. The old
boy tried to shake me off and edge through the French
windows, but it is pretty hard to shake me off when I
am at my best. I grabbed him by the buttonhole and
steered him back into the room. And when, in a dazed
sort of way, he reached out and took a slice of cake, I
knew the battle was won.

"The way I look at it is this," I said, getting between
him and the window. "A man like my uncle would no
doubt have a number of accounts in different banks.
The one on which he drew this cheque happened to have
insufficient funds in it, and the bank-manager, with
gross discourtesy——"

"Well, yes, possibly——"

"I shall tell my uncle of what has occurred——"

At this moment somebody behind me said "Ha!"
or it may have been "Ho!" and I spun round, and
there in the French window was standing another
perfect stranger.

This new addition to our little party was a long, lean,
Anglo-Indian-looking individual. You know the type.

"Your summer-house?" he said in a low, almost reverent voice. The spaciousness of the thing seemed to have affected his vocal chords. "How could he have stolen a summer-house?"

"I don't know how he did it.   In sections, I suppose. It's one of those portable summer-houses.   I had it sent down from the Stores last month.   And there it is, standing at the bottom of his garden.   I tell you the man ought not to be at large.   He's a menace.   Good God!   When I was in Africa during the Boer War a platoon of Australians scrounged one of my cast-iron sheds one night, but I never expected that that sort of thing happened in England in peace-time."

Corky, a sudden bright light shone on me.   I saw all. It was that word "scrounge" that did it.   I remembered now having heard of Australia and its scroungers. They go about pinching things, Corky—— No, I do *not* mean spring suits, I mean things that really matter, things of vital import like sundials and summer-houses —not beastly spring suits which nobody could tell you wanted, anyway, and you'll get it back to-morrow as good as new.

Well, be that as it may, I saw all.

"Sir Edward," I said, "let me explain.   My uncle——"

But it was no use, Corky.   They wouldn't listen. The O.B.E. gave me one look, the Vulture gave me another, and I rather fancy Myrtle gave me a third, and then they pushed off and I was alone.

I went over to the table and helped myself to a bit of cold buttered toast, a broken man.

About ten minutes later there was a sound of cheery whistling outside and the Stepper walked in.

"Here I am, my boy," said the Stepper. "I've got the eggs." And he began shedding them out of every pocket. It looked as if he had been looting every hen-roost in the neighbourhood. "Where are our guests?"

"Gone."

"Gone?"

He looked round.

"Hullo! Where's the furniture?"

"Gone."

"Gone?"

I explained.

"Tut, tut!" said the Stepper.

I sniffed a bit.

"Don't make sniffing noises at me, my boy," said the Stepper, reprovingly. "The best of men have cheques returned from time to time."

"And I suppose the best of men sneak eggs and roses and sundials and summer-houses?" I said. And I spoke bitterly, Corky.

"Eh?" said the Stepper. "You don't mean to say——?"

"I certainly do."

"Tell me all."

I told him all.

"Too bad!" he said. "I never have been able to shake off this habit of scrounging. Wherever Charles Percy Cuthbertson is, there he scrounges. But who would have supposed that people would make a fuss about a little thing like that? I'm disappointed in the old country. Why, nobody in Australia minds a little scrounging. What's mine is yours and what's yours is mine—that's our motto out there. All this to-do about a sundial and a summer-house! Why, bless my soul, I've scrounged a tennis lawn in my time. Oh, well, there's nothing to be done about it, I suppose."

"There's a lot to be done about it," I said. "The O.B.E. doesn't believe I've got an uncle. He thinks I pinched all those things myself."

"Does he?" said the Stepper, thoughtfully. "Does he, indeed?"

"And the least you can do is to go up to the Hall and explain."

"Precisely what I was about to suggest myself. I'll walk over now and put everything right. Trust me, my boy. I'll soon fix things up."

And he trotted out, and that, Corky, is the last I ever saw of him till to-day. It's my belief he never went anywhere near the Hall. I am convinced that he walked straight to the station, no doubt pocketing a couple of telegraph poles and a five-barred gate or so on the way, and took the next train to London. Certainly there was nothing in the O.B.E.'s manner when I met him next day in the village to suggest that everything had been put right and things fixed up. I don't suppose a jute merchant has ever cut anybody so thoroughly.

And that's why I wish to impress it upon you, Corky, old horse, that that bloke, that snaky and conscienceless old Stepper, is best avoided. No matter how glittering the prospects he may hold out, I say to you—shun him! Looking at the thing in one way, taking the short, narrow view, I am out a lunch. Possibly a very good lunch. But do I regret? No. Who knows but that a man like that would have been called to the telephone at the eleventh hour, leaving me stuck with the bill?

And even supposing he really has got money now. How did he get it? That is the question. I shall make inquiries, and if I find that someone has pinched the Albert Memorial I shall know what to think.

THE END

Books by *P. G. Wodehouse*

Eggs, Beans and Crumpets
Uncle Fred in the Springtime
The Code of the Woosters
Summer Moonshine
Lord Emsworth and Others
Laughing Gas
Young Men in Spats
The Luck of the Bodkins
Blandings Castle
Right Ho, Jeeves
Thank You, Jeeves
Heavy Weather
Mulliner Nights
Hot Water
If I Were You
Very Good, Jeeves
Big Money
Summer Lightning
Money for Nothing
Mr. Mulliner Speaking
Meet Mr. Mulliner
Carry On, Jeeves
The Heart of a Goof
Leave it to Psmith
Ukridge
The Inimitable Jeeves
The Coming of Bill
The Girl on the Boat
Jill the Reckless
A Damsel in Distress
Love Among the Chickens
A Gentleman of Leisure
Indiscretions of Archie
Piccadilly Jim
Adventures of Sally
Clicking of Cuthbert
Week-End Wodehouse
Mulliner Omnibus
Jeeves Omnibus

WEEK-END WODEHOUSE

With an Introduction by Hilaire Belloc

Illustrated by Kerr   512 pages   7s. 6d. net

Here, in one delectable volume, is the cream of Wodehouse wit and humour. The best of the short stories, excerpts from the novels, essays, prefaces and humorous articles, not previously printed in book form, make up this book. The whole volume is punctuated with brief snatches of traditional dialogue and gems of Wodehousian description.

"Fulfils to perfection the promise of its title. A brilliant and representative selection."—*Times Literary Supplement*.

"A ravishing anthology."—*Frank Swinnerton*.

"Masses of pleasure unalloyed for everybody."—*Wyndham Lewis*.

"Comfortably substantial, pleasant both to hold and regard. . . . Answers to all that is implicit in its title."—*Scotsman*.

"As good a cross-section of the Master's works as possible. Mr. Wodehouse is the best of doctors, the best of tonics, the best antidote for depression and the income-tax people and dictators."—*Field*.

"Sheer felicity . . . scintillating."—*Truth*.

"If there be mortal who could pick up Wodehousian selections and cast aside after a few days I have yet to meet him . . . I place *Week-end Wodehouse* above the Jeeves and Mulliner omnibuses, and that is high praise indeed."—*Western Morning News*.

Books by P. G. Wodehouse

UNCLE FRED IN THE SPRINGTIME

The Duke of Dunstable was a nobleman of proud and haughty spirit—the last person in the world from whom one could hope to withhold pigs with impunity. Yet the Earl of Emsworth, faced by the appalling prospect of losing his prize pig, the Empress of Blandings, defied him to do his worst and sought an ally in Frederick, fifth Earl of Ickenham. Blandings Castle was shaken to its very foundations before Uncle Fred, overthrowing the dire plan of his powerful adversaries, came out smiling and triumphant. A book of sheer delight.   7s. 6d. net.

"Almost baffles description . . . extraordinarily ingenious."
—*Times Literary Supplement.*

"A brilliant plot . . . as elegant and as satisfying as a complicated chess puzzle."—*Spectator.*

"Mr. Wodehouse in a mood of supremely mettlesome fertility. Decorated everywhere with simile and epigram of genius."—*Frank Swinnerton.*

THE CODE OF THE WOOSTERS

In this absolutely supreme example of Wodehouse genius, Bertie became involved in an imbroglio that tested the Wooster soul as it had seldom been tested before. Only the resources of the inimitable Jeeves saved him from the worst consequences of the sinister affair of the eighteenth-century cow-creamer and the small brown leather-covered notebook.   4s. net.

"One of the best he has written in the last thirty years. A masterpiece in the grand manner."—*Times Literary Supplement.*

"Mr. Wodehouse at his best . . . Bertie Wooster and the incomparable Jeeves have never risen to greater heights of invention."—*Daily Telegraph.*

"Vintage Wodehouse."—*Observer.*

SUMMER MOONSHINE

To Sir Buckstone Abbott, Walsingford Hall was nothing but a blot upon the landscape. It so jarred upon his sensitive soul that it was his avowed intention to unload the unsightly pile on the first prospective buyer. His chance came when the Princess von und zu Dwornitzchek expressed the opinion that the hall was ' cute ' . . . A novel which will reduce the readers to tears of delight. 3s. net.

"Mr. Wodehouse comes once again like sunshine upon a world of apprehensive gloom . . . A source of undiluted pleasure."—*Sunday Mercury*.

"Described with all Mr. Wodehouse's ingenuity and sense of the ridiculous. The absurdities come so pat that it is dangerous to read the book in public."—*Daily Telegraph*.

"A visible miracle of fun."—*Observer*.

LORD EMSWORTH AND OTHERS

Never before has Mr. Wodehouse treated us to so dazzling an assembly of characters—Clarence, ninth Earl of Emsworth; Mr. Mulliner and the jovial company at the Angler's Rest; the indomitable Ukridge; and the greatest of all golfing raconteurs, the Oldest Member. 3s. net.

"Characteristic verbal gems . . . among his best."—*Times*.

"At the top of his form . . . capital entertainment."—*Scotsman*.

"Mr. Wodehouse remains first-class."—*John O' London's Weekly*.

"Continues to make our ribs ache . . . Unbearably funny."—*Observer*.